VALERIE HOLMES

CALEB'S FAITH

Complete and Unabridged

LINFORD
Leicester

First published in Great Britain in 2007

First Linford Edition
published 2008

British Library CIP Data

Holmes, Valerie
  Caleb's faith.—Large print ed.—
  Linford romance library
  1. Love stories
  2. Large type books
  I. Title
  823.9′2 [F]

  ISBN 978–1–84782–223–9

Published by
F. A. Thorpe (Publishing)
Anstey, Leicestershire

Set by Words & Graphics Ltd.
Anstey, Leicestershire
Printed and bound in Great Britain by
T. J. International Ltd., Padstow, Cornwall

This book is printed on acid-free paper

CALEB'S FAITH

Faith Berry's naivety nearly lands her in gaol when she tries to warn a gathered crowd of villagers that the militia is about to arrive to arrest them. Little does she realise that the leaders are not the good men that she had always presumed them to be. Ironically, Major Caleb Kingsby, the man whose plans she had just thwarted, saves her from the resulting mayhem. The resulting chaos splits her family — and changes her life forever.

Books by Valerie Holmes
in the Linford Romance Library:

THE MASTER OF MONKTON
MANOR
THE KINDLY LIGHT
HANNAH OF HARPHAM HALL
PHOEBE'S CHALLENGE
BETRAYAL OF INNOCENCE
AMELIA'S KNIGHT
OBERON'S CHILD
REBECCA'S REVENGE
THE CAPTAIN'S CREEK
MISS GEORGINA'S CURE

1

Faith stared at the strange man with his arms raised to the sky as he stood proudly proclaiming his message before man and God. In his plain dark clothes he was perched on an upturned barrel; his solid silhouette was striking against the clear blue sky. He shouted his words with passion at the gathered throng across the open field. It seemed to Faith that he was a sincere man. She presumed he was of God because he was speaking to the poor and humble, like her, without, it appeared, the need of the security offered by the pulpit, font or walls. Strange, though, she thought that a man would prefer to stand in the open field on such a chilly day as this and speak out to them when he could be in the shelter of the church with better, cleaner folk. People like him were mysteries to her, as she failed

1

to see what they could change by shouting to folk who have no say in the way their lives unfolded. They had to work or starve.

Seeing Clara, her elder sister, sitting pretty on the old gig her husband owned, Faith felt a stab of jealousy; not for the marriage itself but because people treated her sister with greater respect as if she was somehow accepted into the village society.

The village had changed a lot in the last ten years. When she was a girl it was just a nestle of little cottages and farm holdings. Now, there were tall houses lining the road. Some of the old cottages had been emptied and pulled down, leaving only a few of the originals on the outskirts of the village. Their mother looked upon Clara with great pride because she had, in her parents' viewpoint, married well. Her husband, Daniel Dell, was the only son of the cooper's and had inherited enough money to invest in the new housing. Clara had a secure home, a respectable house in the middle of the village's new row. The new stretch of road was even surfaced in something hard and the people who lived there could walk along a raised paved pathway to the cluster of newly built, bay fronted shops. Soon, Faith thought, the village would be lost to them and only fancy folk would be allowed to walk there lest the commoners bring in too much mud and dirt. 'Commoners' was how they were becoming known. It was a term that referred to everyone who lived in the old cottages across the common away from the new housing.

However, despite her mother's strong affection for Clara, Faith thought her to be an absolute snob as she rarely visited them anymore and did not come and play with her other two younger sisters, Jane and Sarah.

Faith looked down at her own feet and shook her head. She rubbed the back of her boots on the grass to remove some of the mud gathered from the lengthy walk through the woods to the village. Then she replaced Clara's old bonnet back square on her dark-blonde hair. One day, Faith thought, I'll have a gig and a bonnet of my own, and I'll still see Ma as often as I can. She straightened out her faded skirts, in case Clara should deign to acknowledge her, because despite what she thought of Clara, Faith did not want to let her sister down, even if she did think her a snob — family was family after all. But her sister didn't even look around to see if they were there. She was, like everyone else, fascinated by the speaker's fiery words.

'See, Faith, how even the better folk come and listen to him. He's truly a man of God! So wise and fair, I wish your father was here to see him. If there were more prepared to listen to him, life would be so much easier for us village folk.' Her mother's eyes almost appeared to light up as she spoke. Faith nodded her agreement which pleased her mother. However, she did not understand why her ma should be so impressed by the presence of a few gigs, a coach and two wagons carrying what looked like a collection of local gentry. It all seemed strange to Faith. Why should the better off come to the field and listen when they could attend a church or invite the man into their own estates? It was almost as if they were not in fact listening to him at all but watching who was in the crowd. Faith suddenly had an uncomfortable feeling of being penned in by these strange people and their vehicles. She shrugged her shoulders and thought she was being fanciful again — as Ma would say. She looked at her mother who was still completely absorbed in the man's words. What did words like equality, men born equal, fair wages and shorter hours have to do with the Bible? He looked like a preacher and certainly sounded as if he was preaching to them. However, as she listened to his speech the tempo changed, the messages were far harder and what he was doing felt very wrong to Faith. The men near him were becoming noisier as they agreed and cheered his every word. Faith tried to listen, and take in what he said but his message appeared distant to her. He was promising them good earthly souls, as he called them, victory after a long hard fight. He said they were living in hell as a reward for their labour. What fight was he talking about? Faith thought that his words were getting dangerously near stirring up bad feelings against those who paid them need.

Her mother's eyes settled once more on Clara, 'Soon you will find a husband and be on your own gig, Faith. You are pretty and strong, with a quick wit — but, child, hold that tongue of yours. A good man does not like a sharp tongue in a pretty head.'

Faith thought about literally holding her tongue but decided that would be childish. 'I'm not old enough to wed yet, Ma!' Faith muttered indignantly, feeling sorry for Clara because she had to sleep and do . . . well 'things', whatever 'things' were, with Daniel Dell. This was not something Faith felt at all envious of because she thought him to be a drunken boor.

'Oh, Faith, you are more than ready for a husband. Look at you! You've a fine body and could bear a man many fine children. You don't need all that nonsense of the well-to-do. There was a time when my mother and her grandmother were caught up in introductions and coming out. Those days are long since gone.' She looked down and sighed.

'Love?' Faith suggested. 'What about falling in love?'

Her mother sighed and looked at her, 'Love does not feed a hungry belly, child!' she said sharply.

'Then why create more hungry bellies to feed by getting wed? And besides, I thought you said I was no longer a child!' Faith replied indignantly.

Her mother ignored her comments, which was her way when she had no

7

better answer. 'Your Pa will find you a man who will provide you with a good home of your own. Then you'll understand what is important and what are just fanciful notions.' The woman smiled at her, her eyes filled with hope at the prospect. Faith's heart felt like breaking. She loved her mother dearly but at times she appeared almost too simple in her assumptions. How easily she found pleasure in the knowledge that she had a home and children, yet nothing else to speak of, like a loving partner. Where would she find the one thing that Faith could not bear the thought of marrying without — a true sincere man who would love her? Could they not afford to find that too? Did she have to settle for a life in a tiny cottage, giving birth and seeing her own babies struggle to survive in this harsh world? Her only other function would be to be there for the whim of a man of her father's choice, but not of hers. Faith did not answer her but shrank back. There had to be more to life than that!

Her mother tugged at her hand. She had obviously thought of an answer for her. 'Rich people have to marry people who their fathers think are suitable for them and princes have to marry princesses. So, love and marriage have really no import at all.' Her mother smiled broadly, pleased that she had, for once, answered her outspoken daughter with a retort she could not challenge.

Faith shrugged, conceding her mother's point which pleased her tremendously. However, she watched the men who had stopped working in the fields, the mill and those who had suspended their trades to listen to the stranger's speech and wondered if this bold act was lost on him. Still, it had meant that she had respite from her own chores.

She and her mother had only walked to the village to sell their eggs, gloves, and whatever else they had prepared with hours of labour — they and the girls tried to produce as many things as they could in their modest home on the

9

edge of the village — and to meet her father. Faith's family home had to be at a distance because of the smell from the dyeing process they used on the skins their father bought from the butcher's. Preparing the leather and wool was a pungent process so they lived a life separate, most of the time, yet were needed by these people to trade with. The villagers were friendly to them, as they exchanged goods regularly, but Faith always felt like an outsider. Her mother did not, or if she did her cheerful manner never betrayed her true feelings.

Today her father had said that they must meet him in the village. Faith was excited by this because he was not a man who spent much time with his family. He always had 'business', her mother said by means of excuse, but when he eventually returned home his business appeared to have made him drunk.

'Ma, should we not be on our way into the village? Won't Father be waiting for us?' Faith was hoping she could encourage her mother to leave now because her father was not a man to be kept waiting. She hated it when he rebuked her mother in front of them. She was so submissive to him.

Her mother looked at her as if her words were somehow drifting into her mind slowly. She sensed how much her mother really wanted to stay and listen to the stranger's talk. But Faith was becoming worried by the way the man was stirring up bad feelings within the hearts of the workers.

'Yes, my dear, you are quite right. We shall have to leave.' She stared back at the speaker. 'Doesn't he speak in the most lovely way?' she said. 'Yes, quite special — every word filled with passion.'

Trouble was the word that came to Faith's mind.

'I really believe he is blessed; so brave to stand and speak his mind in front of all of us strangers.' Her mother clasped her hand and started to walk away.

'He's been educated, Ma. Those kind all speak the same way . . . properly,' Faith said, not really impressed because how were folk to know where you were from if you didn't speak in your native dialect? Mind, Faith had to admit that some of the traders who travelled the length of the country were really difficult to understand. She presumed they must have foreign blood in them because they hardly seemed to be able to make themselves understood.

'I hope that our Clara will not be offended that we have not waited to pass some time with her.' Her mother was looking at her eldest daughter with the usual pride showing in her expression. 'Daniel is a fine man. She is so very lucky.'

'I should think she will find it in her heart to forgive us if we leave without speaking to her. Perhaps Father will allow us to visit her whilst we are all in town.' Faith's sarcasm was lost on her mother who agreed with the statement and also agreed they might all be able to call upon her in her new house. Clara could do no wrong in her mother's eyes. She did not even notice how Clara shifted uneasily whenever they were seen together in the village. Clara's clothes seemed to become finer with each visit, which meant that Ma and her had been given her cast offs to wear. Ma was thrilled with this and at her daughter's generosity. Faith smiled because in truth no one could change her mother's view of her eldest daughter, she always saw the good in everyone, even in her father. But she wondered why Clara had not presented her mother with something new to wear. The thought never even passed her mother's mind.

2

Faith led her mother away from the massed people. She could tell by the hesitation in her step that the older woman really wanted to stay. She could not understand why Clara had not invited her mother to go with her. Surely she was not ashamed to be seen sitting next to her? They left the crowd, making their way carefully back on to the road. There they had the choice to walk either upon the rough grass and moss covered verge, or down the middle of the rutted road in order to go around the parked coach.

Faith steered her mother carefully along the verge. She would rather collect mud on her boots than be knocked down by a passing vehicle, or break her ankle in one of the cart ruts. As they walked by the side of the fine coach Faith glanced up and saw several well dressed men engaged in an animated discussion within it. One glowered at her for even daring to glance inside their opulent world. Instantly, she diverted her attention elsewhere, looking up to the driver's seat. He was a mature man who appeared to be cold, even though he had wrapped a large blanket around his overcoat. He also looked bored by events, unmoved by the passion of the speaker. However, the man next to him was wearing a greatcoat, hat, scarf and gloves. He saw her staring at them and, unlike the fellow passenger within the coach, he smiled down at her. He was much younger than the driver and she could not help but admire his dark features. The window was open so Faith listened innocently to the snippet of conversation that spilled out of the coach. She did this whenever her father talked in hushed tones to her mother. It was how she had found out that Daniel Dell had proposed to Clara before it was agreed or announced to the whole family.

'Where are they?' snapped an angry voice from within the vehicle.

'The militia will arrive shortly — trust me, and don't worry so, Gerald. They may be newly formed but they are trained men coming from good stock, disciplined. Mostly they are soldiers returned from the wars. They know how to fight. Believe me! This rabble will be split up within the hour and the leaders thrown behind bars where they belong. They are no match for trained soldiers.' The man who replied had a calm and well educated voice. 'No need to concern yourself. It will be sorted out this day. Some of the wretches will swing and the others we'll send to America. You mark my word!'

'America doesn't want them anymore. Bloody colonials! They don't appreciate the free labour we send out to them. Well they don't value their homeland any more, do they? We'll ship them to Cook's country instead. That'll be far enough. It takes rabble like them to tame a new nation.'

Someone from inside the coach laughed, which made Faith quicken her step. How could they destroy the lives of men and their families so easily, without having any conscience? She was both livid and frightened by the men's callous attitude. These people were not rabble, they were the villagers. Her own neighbours. Faith's face must have showed her disgust because the smile on the face of the man atop the coach faded, and Faith felt scared that she had offended him also. She was in no position to stand up against any of them — they were gentry and had power. Neither did she have any wish to be sent anywhere across the vast oceans.

Looking straight ahead of her she could see the bend in the road up ahead. Faith linked arms with her mother and swiftly walked her forwards beyond the stationary coach and around the curve in the road until they

17

were out of sight. 'Whatever is the matter with you, child? At this rate the eggs will be scrambled by the time we arrive!'

'Ma,' Faith whispered into her mother's ear. 'The militia are coming here. I've got to warn the people back there. You run on to tell Pa what is happening and I'll catch you up. Don't worry about me. I'll just tell them that they're in danger and then I'll follow on after you.' Faith saw her mother's lip tremble slightly. The woman wanted to stop her but, on this occasion, she could not. Faith took a step toward the field once more as her mother grabbed her arm in one last desperate attempt.

'Faith! Think of the danger you could be in. What of our Clara? What will happen to her if she's caught up in a scuffle with the soldiers?' The panic on her mother's face touched Faith deeply. She idolized her daughter. 'She's a lady, lass, she don't belong in there.'

'Ma, go to Pa, like I said, and I'll tell Clara to get home as soon as possible.

Please do not bring attention to yourself or I shall be in a lot of trouble for spoiling their plans.' She shooed the woman along, stopping her from speaking further. 'Quickly, Ma! Don't worry, I'll be fine. All I have to do is spread the word.'

'Take care, Faith. Stay with Clara. Be safe!' Her mother's words faded away as, without thinking of her own safety, Faith ran back into the field and to the outskirts of the crowd.

She headed straight for the speaker upon the barrel. If she told one of his men then they could pass the word to him and everyone would be warned. They'd have time to clear and all would be back to normal again. The man who was still speaking was even closer to her now. His words were gaining momentum. Gone were the Bible references. Now he had the crowd before him in his enigmatic power he was openly criticizing the land owners and all who took a man's labour for little pay. The Regent himself came in for attack as did his mad father. The opulence in which they lived and the amount they spent on wine and finery enraged the working men. This was what these people wanted. She could see their satisfaction as the crowd jeered and hissed at the figures quoted. They were so large that they lost meaning to Faith because she could not imagine how any person could consume so much value in drink. It all seemed dangerously far-fetched. Next, the mill owners were also named as leeches of honest men. These were indeed rebellious words and the people who listened seemed unaware of the web they were being drawn into. His speech was instilling anger and hatred into the worker's minds. This, Faith realized, was very daring indeed and no matter what truth lay behind them they could cause death to innocent simple-minded folk who were being duped by this unusual spectacle.

The passion with which the orator shouted out his message scared her. She walked slowly over to a man with a bludgeon standing near him. At first he stared at her as if she was a threat, but then he saw the concern on her face and raised a questioning eyebrow.

'What do yer want, lassie?' the man said in his gruff voice.

'Sir, the militia have been sent for. They aim to disperse the crowd and arrest you and your friends.' Faith had hardly spoken the words when two men standing nearest her, who had overheard her warning, turned and immediately shouted to the crowd.

'Flee! Flee! Soldiers!' Instantly, all about her were in panic. The speaker was lifted bodily from the barrel by the men with bludgeons and carried off.

'What about warning everyone?' she shouted, but they paid her no heed as they took him to a group of horses that were tied to a tree nearby. They were gone in an instant. The men and women left in the field seemed to come to their senses as the man's spell was broken and reality returned. They started to run in all directions as the first of the militia men rode into view across the fields. A small group of soldiers split off to follow the riders, the others rode straight toward the crowd. She heard them shouting at people to stand still, but panic ensued. Faith was now at the front of the crowd. She tried to run against the flow of the frightened people in order to reach Clara's gig. She had not gone more than half way across the field when Daniel Dell crossed her path.

'Daniel! Daniel!' Faith shouted, as she was pushed from one body into another as people jostled past her. He glanced over his shoulder, saw her, but did not even hesitate in his stride. Instead, he appeared to increase his speed, climbed upon the gig and snapped the reins sprightly. In no time they were on the road and travelling swiftly beyond the waiting coach.

Faith thought that she saw Clara looking over her shoulder as if searching for her but she could not be sure, for within minutes she felt a hefty push in her back and was knocked to the ground. Faith curled into a tight ball as either man or horse ran over her. She wrapped her arms around her head fearing for her life. She thought a shot rang out but she dared not look up. It was no use, she would have to stay put or die if she moved whilst the mêlée carried on over and about her. Faith realised she could be arrested, or . . . she knew not what else would befall her.

She tried to control her breath which had quickened, her throat tightened as if an invisible hand of fear had caused it to close slightly. Waiting for a moment's pause in the noise surrounding her she dared to look up. A few feet from her lay the broken body of a man she recognised from the next village. His unseeing eyes stared directly at her. Had his own people run him down, or the militia?

Soldiers had caught a few men in the distance and still they followed the slower, older members of the throng until they tired on their way to return to their homes. She knelt up. Swaying she flinched as a stabbing pain shot across her body, her ribs felt so sore where she had been trodden upon. It was hard but slowly she stood as straight as she could holding her arm to her side to give it some comfort and support.

Faith took two steps forward and stumbled falling heavily. As she fell back to the ground she saw the coach pull away. She wondered if they were proud of themselves or had enjoyed the morning's sport. How long would it be before the militiamen found her lying there? She cringed at the thought and fought the urge to cry. She could not call out for help for fear of attracting them. How could her day . . . her life, have gone so completely wrong within the space of an hour? She'd only wanted to help them; yet, nobody had helped her — not even her own brother-in-law, Daniel.

Faith gasped as a firm hand was placed on her back. 'Oh God,' she cried, 'Someone help me.'

3

Faith struggled to stand up. She was aware that her dress was covered in mud. How could she stagger into town looking like this? Her mother would panic and her father would rebuke her for being so stupid as to place herself in such a position, and the soldiers, if they were still there, could accuse her of being involved. Her usually clean hair was spattered with dirt too. Why hadn't Daniel stopped? He must have seen her.

She was momentarily confused and stared at the wet grass around her. Then, as the hand moved from her, she remembered she had been discovered and her hands gripped the tuffs of grass as if she could fight to be left alone. She could not.

Two strange arms lifted her up to her feet by looping under hers and bodily bringing her upright. She tried not to make a sound, but could not stop herself from squealing, as her side hurt her so much. She wanted to behave with dignity even if she looked like a dirty scrap of humanity.

'I've done nothing wrong. Let me go!' Faith felt desperation rising within and swallowed hard trying to keep some modicum of composure.

'Miss, if I do that you'll be in the lock-up before nightfall. You're coming with me. I shall see you are tended to. What possessed you to interfere?' She was swept off her feet and swung up into the muscular arms of a stranger. He was strong and, as she looked into his face, she stared up into the deep brown eyes of the man who had been sitting next to the driver. He carried her in his arms as if she was no burden to him at all. There was no vehicle to be seen by the roadside. Faith could not see how he was to help her if they had no means of escape.

'Listen to me, miss. I need you to

stay still and quiet.' He placed her carefully down behind a dry stone wall sheep pen. Normally they were used to give the sheep a place to shelter in bad weather. It was a cold and damp place. As he whispered to her, 'Remember, stay still and not a word just for a few moments,' he winked at her.

Then he turned his back to her and sat down upon the wall, letting the length of his coat fall over her. Moments later she heard horses' hooves approaching along the road.

A man stopped and spoke to him. 'We've looked everywhere, sir, they've gone. Have you seen anyone run down there?'

'No, I think you scared them all off.' His voice sounded very calm to Faith. 'Did you see which way they headed, Sergeant?' He obviously was not daunted by speaking to the soldier in such an easy manner.

'No, sir. It has been a bit disappointing really. The speaker and his rabble have escaped . . . again. I tell you, if I find out who warned them off this time I'll kick their hide black and blue!' He coughed. 'Pardon, sir, I'll lock them up with the blackguards anyhow. Someone is in his pay, or a keen supporter. These people will bring down the country. I tell you, if they have their way there will be guillotines in every market town square, just like over in France. They don't know when they're well off!' The man sounded really angry. Faith stayed stock still, not daring to change position in the slightest.

'Sergeant, I'm sure their word will lose impact in time. Englishmen have no stomach for Madame Guillotine. You go and enjoy a drink in the tap room. Make sure you warn everyone you rounded up before you release them.' The stranger, Faith thought, spoke to them with such confidence and ease. He must have some authority over the militia, but then if he did, why on earth would he help her?

'Aye, I hope you're right, Caleb, sir, but those who think they know better than us say they're a real danger to us. We need to catch them or there'll be more laws put through to stop the meetings, that will mean more people will suffer.' The man paused for a moment, and then asked Caleb, 'Where is your horse or carriage?'

'I told the driver to go on back to the house. My guests were becoming uncomfortable.' He paused and then added, 'They will be disappointed. They were baying for blood.'

'Aye, no doubt if they got their hands on the one who warned them this time they'd string 'em up. Why are you waiting here?'

'I decided to stay a while before going into the village. I fancy some exercise before I face their inquisition over what went wrong.'

'I can understand that, sir. Well, you've a good day for a walk, but take care, man. If they're around here they won't question who you are. They see anyone wearing decent clothes as the enemy of the common man. They'll target you without question.'

'Aye, perhaps they would given the chance. Thank you, James, for your concern. I shall be fine because they have long gone from here.'

'Well, Caleb, I've got to go and report in — Your statement 'they won't be happy' is slightly underestimating the situation I feel. God help you, sir. I shall tell them you are exhausting all possibilities before returning.' The man coughed loudly then Faith heard the horses move off. At first the stranger did not move, then, as if he had suddenly remembered she was there, he swung his legs around and jumped down onto the ground next to her.

'Miss, I'm so sorry to leave you like this. Can you stand up?'

She could hear the concern in his voice as she tried to sit up. Her side hurt her so much that she winced before she could answer him.

'Obviously not,' he said, and helped her to straighten up. 'What is your name?' he asked her.

'Faith Berry,' she replied. 'Who are you, sir?'

'Caleb Kingsby, miss. You are related to Clara, Dell's wife?' He stated the fact as if he already knew who she was. There was a sharpness to his tone that surprised her.

'Yes, I'm her sister. Do you know her?' Faith asked, thinking if he did, she would find out all about him from her sister when she was fit to visit her. Perhaps if he could take her to their house she could be cleaned up and tended there.

'I shall have to leave you here whilst I fetch a means of transport,' he told her. 'Unfortunately, it will not be comfortable, but we can hardly leave you in a field.'

'Can you take me to Clara's house, please? I'm sure she would be pleased to help me.' Faith looked up at him as he removed his greatcoat and wrapped it around her as she leaned against the wall.

'No, but I'll see you safe. I doubt

whether Daniel Dell would help anyone, if you will pardon my being so outspoken on the subject. I tend to speak as I find and I find you amazingly brave and naïve to do what you did . . . bordering on the point of stupidity.'

Faith was shocked that he should say such a thing. 'The militia were coming . . . as you knew.'

'Yes, I knew it and, if you had not intervened, four evil men would have been locked away. Instead, they ride off to cause yet more unrest and suffering to unsuspecting people. But you were not to realise this.'

She stared at his face, looking into the depth of his eyes. 'They were trying to help the poor, weren't they?' she asked, not understanding the situation at all.

'No, they weren't. They dupe the poor for their own ends. However, I do not intend to stand here explaining politics to a young lady in distress . . . '

'Even though it was caused by her own misdeeds?' she asked and saw his mouth turn up at the corners into a sympathetic grin.

'In this instance . . . yes. Stay here, I shall not be too long as I have a horse at the inn not two miles away. I shall return swiftly and retrieve both you and my coat. Do not be frightened, I shall keep my word. Besides, I have to return as you do have my coat.' He smiled at her in a friendly, reassuring manner before he walked off at a pace along the road.

*   *   *

The gig was moving at quite a speed as it travelled along the road, passing by Flora Berry as she tried to make her way swiftly to the village without breaking her precious eggs.

'Clara! Clara, my dear child!' Flora shouted, but thought she had not been heard by them, when the vehicle was pulled to a halt at the side of the road ahead of her.

She quickened her step and saw

Daniel jump down and wave at her. She smiled warmly at him. He was such a fine young man. Clara had done so well, she thought.

'You'll have to squeeze in, Ma Berry,' he said brightly.

That was no problem for Flora's slight build. He took hold of her basket and glanced inside it. 'Clara, we'll be having fresh eggs this night, look what your Ma's brought for us.' He placed the basket on Clara's lap as he climbed back in and collected the reins.

Flora did not know what to say. She flushed deeply because they were not to be gifts. They were meant to be sold, like the gloves.

'Ma, were they really for us?' Clara asked.

'Well, who else does she have living in the village?' Daniel answered, and shook his head at his wife.

Flora had no choice. She had to say it. 'Of course they are, dear.'

Clara put her arm around her mother's thin waist and hugged her close. Flora's heart lifted but what she would tell her husband she didn't rightly know. Then she remembered about Faith.

'Daniel, did you see Faith before you left the field? She ran back to warn you two that there was going to be trouble. Mind, I don't know why because that man had the most lovely voice I've ever heard.'

Clara looked at Daniel, who shrugged his shoulders and Flora noticed the girl's colour flushed red. Clara was so sensitive, Flora thought. She truly cared for them all.

'I didn't see her but the soldiers told them all to move on so I suppose she's making her way back to the village as we speak.' He turned back to look at Flora and gave her a reassuring smile. Then his eyes glanced down at the basket again. 'You've been fetching Clara new gloves, Ma?'

This time Flora spoke out. She couldn't let them have the gloves as well. That would be too much, even ough she would dearly have loved to. Flora looked at Clara and said softly, 'I have to sell them, Clara. You do understand, don't you?'

'Yes, of course I do. Daniel is teasing you, Ma. I have enough gloves of my own. Mother has been generous enough with the eggs. Here . . . ' she held out the pair of freshly made gloves to Flora and the woman grasped them tightly whilst smiling humbly at her.

'Well, Ma, if you do sell them, please try and be discreet. It will do Clara's reputation no good at all to have her mother peddling goods on a street corner. Perhaps you could go to the milliners and see if she'll buy them from you.' Daniel said in his authorative voice.

'Yes, Daniel, I will. It is an excellent idea,' Flora promised, as she would never knowingly do anything that would cause them embarrassment. Then she glanced back along the road.

'Are you sure we should not return and look for Faith? She could be in trouble . . . '

'Ma, stop your worrying. She's a big girl and can look after herself. Send Pa to look for her if she's not back in the village. Right now my priority is to see you two ladies safely back. Did you say that she went back to warn us?'

'Yes, she heard that the militia men were being sent in and ran back to tell people. I told her to find you firstly and stay with you,' Flora added.

He grinned and flicked the horses' reins. 'So it was our own little Faith who told Gibbons to split. Well, well,' he muttered.

Flora looked up at Daniel's strong features and realised she was being a worry-bucket as Faith called her. He was right of course; Pa would sort everything out if she had got mixed up in the trouble. Daniel was such a level headed man, that Flora felt loved and protected by his care. Her Faith was so brave. She chatted to Clara as they made the rest of the journey to the village. Flora was relieved that she could not see Pa anywhere in the village

..are. He must still be in the Falcon
..nn. She hoped that this would give her
time to sell the gloves on before he
arrived. If she could get a little more for
them then she may not have to own up
to giving the eggs away.

Clara stepped down and waited for
her mother to follow her. Despite her
used clothes her mother knew how to
hold herself with poise and style. Daniel
took the gig around to the stable block
whilst the women went indoors.

'Clara, I need my basket, pet,' Flora
said nervously.

'Oh Ma, come on in a minute.' The
two women entered the fine hall of the
house. A maid came to greet Clara. She
was only a simple village girl, but never
the less, she was a maid and that was
one more thing that Clara had to add to
her status in the village.

'Molly, take these eggs to the kitchen
and fetch the basket back when it is
empty. Prepare a cup of hot chocolate
and bring some cake or biscuits.' The
girl took hold of the basket, dipped a

crude curtsey and left them.

'Clara, I need to go and . . . '

'Sell your gloves.' She put her hand in her purse. 'Here, take this.' She offered her some coins. 'That is more than you would have been paid for the eggs and the gloves together. If Pa would stop his drinking and look after his family you wouldn't have to disgrace yourself like this.' She put her hand up as Flora was about to protest and placed the money in her mother's pocket. 'I am going to ask Daniel to arrange for Sarah and Jane to be placed in the Dame School. Perhaps then they will find positions or husbands when the time is ripe for them. The vicar's son, Peter, is a year or two older than Sarah. Perhaps she could turn his head a little next time she sees him in church. You need to plan these things; plant seeds that will grow in time. I didn't achieve my own position by spending every available moment sewing gloves around a pathetic candle lamp and flickering fire. You have to be seen in the right places by the

.c people. Now I am established in .e village — and make no mistake, Mama, the village will be a town in time — I can use my influence to help you and the girls out. You should come down here and I'll have a new dress made for you and, as for Faith,' she sighed as she spoke, 'if she hasn't got herself into a heap of trouble I shall see if Daniel can find her a husband, as Pa seems unable to do this simple task. It is time our family improved itself!'

Flora was about to speak when the maid returned with her empty basket and a tray on which there was a porcelain cup filled with an aromatic drink of hot chocolate. Flora took it off her gratefully but Clara dismissed the girl curtly and stared at her mother.

'Thank you, Clara. You really are most thoughtful.' Flora sipped the warm liquid feeling loved and cared for. Everything that Clara said made perfect sense to her. She was so relieved that she would not have to explain anything to Pa. Now she had the money, a warm

drink and Clara was taking steps t.
assure their futures. If she had the time
she might still sell the gloves then she
would have extra money for the first
time in ages. The thought, like the hot
liquid, warmed her. Life, to Flora, was
improving daily, although she did
wonder what was taking Faith so long
to catch up with them.

4

Faith hugged the great coat to her. For a few moments she did nothing but stay put curled up tightly in a ball holding her sides, scared that the soldiers would return. After what seemed to her like ages, yet was no more than the space of a half hour, she dared to move and was relieved that the sharp pain had subsided to a dull ache. With this momentary relief she kneeled up and peeped over the dry stone wall. The road was completely empty, as was the field. Other than the marks of churned ground from the horses' hooves, no one would be any the wiser of what had occurred there this morning. As Faith stood straight, a sharp stab reminded her that all was not as it should be. She pulled the coat on and felt the warmth of this well-made garment. Instinctively, she put her hands into the deep pockets. It was not her intention to pry. However, her hand found the purse that was within it. It was quite heavy. She glanced around her and seeing that no one was approaching she opened it and stared inside. Faith counted more than four guineas before tying it securely and dropping it back where she had found it. That was more money than she had ever seen in her life before. Her father's purse was never as heavy as that despite his business. Next she pulled out a knife that had a leather sheaf that fitted over the blade and hooked onto the handle. The handle was well worn. She placed that also back into the pocket. Her other hand explored the depth of the other pocket and found a folded piece of paper. Again she looked around before daring to open it. No one was in view. She studied the words carefully on the list. It was difficult for her to make out the names, but she had been taught by her mother to know her alphabet, words from the Bible and even write some in the earth with a stick. However, it was always when her father was nowhere around, which was quite often. He did not agree with women being schooled at all. She stared at the words and could determine that it was a list of four people. The second one was *Daniel Dell* — that name stood out. There was another familiar name on there that made her gasp — *Joseph Berry*. The other two were unknown to her but she could just make them out to be *Simeon Huthwaite and Selwyn Gibbons*. She could not understand why the stranger should have her father's name and Daniel's in his pocket. She folded it back up and returned it to where she had found it. Faith was very scared. She had to go to the village and tell her mother what had happened and ask her who these other people were.

She made her way back to the road and started the long walk back towards the village. Faith was grateful for the warmth of the coat. It was not long before a rider appeared in front of her sitting upon a fine chestnut horse. She had no time or energy to hide. It was only then that she realised that she could be accused of stealing the coat and, of course, the money. Either offence would be a hanging one. How much more trouble could she find herself in, in one day?

It was with mixed relief that she saw the figure of the man that the soldier had called Caleb. He did not look at all pleased to see her stumbling along the road towards him. Not waiting for the horse to stop he dismounted and walked the animal the last few feet towards her.

'So, is this how you obey my orders and thank me for helping you? Walking boldly along in the open, whilst wearing my coat is not the most sensible thing to do, woman!' He stared at her, and she knew she must look a really awful sight. 'Do you have a wish to be in trouble or just a natural ability to attract it?'

'I need to find my mother. She will

be worried about me and I must find out if Clara is safe.' She looked up at his dark features. He seemed to be totally unmoved by her words. 'My father is waiting for me in town. He will not be pleased if I am late.' The last statement was added to try to give her actions more credence. However, she could tell he was less impressed by the mention of her father than the previous reasons for leaving her place of shelter.

'Your mother was seen in Dell's gig with your sister Clara. Your father was at the inn, inebriated as usual, but has since left.' He paused and looked around them. 'Strange, but I can't see him here, tearing the countryside apart in search of his wife and daughters. Yet, the inn is abuzz with gossip of the dramatic events that occurred here.' There was open mockery in his voice that could not help but leave her feeling ashamed at her own father's inappropriate behaviour.

Faith stared defiantly at him. 'He will have gone to the village to make sure that mother is safe.' Faith swallowed because she was lying, trying to claw back a modicum of respect for her parent, and they both knew it.

'Let's not waste any more time here on fantasy.' He took the coat back off her and put it on. His hand felt in the pocket as if he had just remembered that his purse was within it. He glanced at her and she felt her cheeks flush. There was a slight grin on one side of his mouth.

'If I intended to steal from you, sir, I would hardly have tramped along in the open for all to see.' She folded her arms indignantly then instantly regretted it because of her bruised ribs. As soon as she flinched, he moved toward her. 'You may have little respect for my father but please do not judge the rest of my family by his individual flaws.'

'Listen, miss, I will judge each member of your family as their own person. I can see you are nothing like your sister Clara.'

'I am muddied, sir, because I fell

down. My sister is . . . '

'Faith Berry, I am well aware of what your sister is. The comment was meant as a compliment to you. Please, place more faith in me if I am to help you.' He grinned at her as he placed a supportive arm around her shoulders and brought her toward the horse's side. 'It would appear that I am destined to.'

'That's my name, Faith,' she said, feeling stupid because he already knew it to be so. She was nervous of him and the animal. Standing by its side she realised how high up she would be on its back. Despite her apprehension he carefully raised her up so that she was sitting across the saddle. Her skirts were bunched up, leaving her feeling exposed and vulnerable. He swung up behind her.

'Try to rest your body against mine and keep your back straight. I'll make the journey as short as possible but it will be more than a touch uncomfortable.' He kicked the horse forwards.

'Shouldn't we be going the other way?' Faith glanced up and saw the stern look on his face.

'Why?' he asked.

'Because . . . the village is that way. So is the inn,' Faith answered, aware that she was stating the obvious, her concern having no impact upon her.

'Indeed, they are, but you are not going to either. I will take you to a place where you can be helped and where you will be out of harm's way.' He pulled the reins and directed the horse's steps onto a track that traversed a field.

'Where are you taking me then? I am not your prisoner, sir. I have rights!' Faith was starting to become frightened. 'What are you? Who are you?'

'I am taking you to a convent where the nuns will nurse you and give you basic, decent food. You will be safe and I will know where to find you when I need you. You forfeited your normal rights, Faith, when you decided to place yourself between the militia and the rabble rousers.' His voice was quite stern.

'What are you? Why do you presume to have the right to kidnap me?' She tried to wriggle but it was impossible. Her side hurt so and there was no means of escape. She could not jump down and run away from this man. Even knowing about the knife, she could hardly use it and overcome his strength in her current condition.

'I am Caleb Kingsby. I own the Falcon Inn, the stables and Kemble Park where the militia has been recently formed.' He looked down into her frightened eyes and added, 'I am the man who stupidly let down his guard to help a well-meaning female who eaves-drops and thinks she can become Robin Hood with ease, and who stupidly left this in his pocket.' He pulled out the piece of folded paper between two fingers. 'Can you read, Faith Berry?'

In the distance she could see the grey building of Bystone Abbey nestled in the valley and surrounded by trees, a gentle stream running by a small garden where two of the nuns bent double could be seen tending their plants. 'I never have been to Dame School, Mr Kingsby.' She was distracted by the peaceful vision ahead of her. Never had she even been aware of its existence. Even so, it could be only seen as the most beautiful prison that she could imagine. She did not belong there and yet there she was destined to be incarcerated. She stopped tears from flowing as the thought gripped her.

'That isn't what I asked, Faith. Now, I shall ask you one last time then our trust will be either complete or broken.' He held the paper in front of her. 'Can you read this? Did you read this?'

'I don't understand any of this. Why have you written my father's name on it? What has Daniel done that you would carry his name also on your person and who are the other two men named? What gives you the right to lock me up in there?' She pointed to the abbey.

'I have the right because no one will find you there. You will have disappeared as if whisked away by the militia or the rabble. But you will be well tended and, when it is safe, I shall return and discuss your family with you. For now, put your energy into recuperating your strength and pondering how it is better to think before acting on impulse.' He held her to him; there was not going to be any way of breaking free.

'My mother will be so worried about me,' she said quietly.

'Your mother will be fine. She will be told that you were seen talking to the speaker, and have had to hide away for a while. They will believe you are staying on a farm, protected by friends of his until this trouble has blown over.' He nodded as if the story sounded plausible.

'They'll want to know where and with whom.' Faith was trying desperately to persuade him that the plan he had worked out was flawed . . . but she knew it wasn't.

'They may want to know but they will be told in no uncertain terms that you were lucky not to end up in gaol and if they want to see you again they should be grateful and stay quiet.' He stopped the horse in front of the large doors and gently slid her to the ground. Then he jumped down at her side placing a strong arm around her shoulders to support her weight.

She stared at him, her hands trembling. 'Please, don't do this. Tell me what it is that my father has done wrong because I can help Mother. She is fragile and the two girls need her and me. Please, don't destroy my family, Mr Kingsby.'

He placed a hand on her shoulder and his manner changed from harshness to one of comparative warmth. 'I believe,' he glanced at the cross above the abbey, 'I do believe you are innocent of all except being naïve, gullible and perhaps a little curious. I do not wish you to be involved in this mess. I saw you risk your own life in order to warn those people that the authorities were coming. What you failed to see in your innocence and stupidity was that the perpetrators of this meeting are dangerous men. Paid to rouse the crowds and cause anarchy. They do not want justice or a fair wage. They want to destroy the nation. I am taking up valuable time seeing to your safety, miss. Have faith in me as I have placed it in you, and be strong again.'

The large doors opened and he turned to face them. A nun stood there in her humble habit. She looked upon Faith and smiled at her kindly.

'This lady has injured ribs. Will you please look after her well and keep her safely within these walls?' He led Faith by the hand to the woman who held out hers to her. Then he placed the purse in the nun's hand, which surprised both women. 'This shall cover any costs you incur.'

'Yes, we will. Thank you, Major

Kingsby; she shall have the best of care that we can offer.'

Caleb nodded, leaving a speechless Faith watching him as he mounted and rode off back towards the town.

5

Faith was shown inside the abbey. As she expected, it was entirely built in stone. She was hoping that the interior was going to be at least draped with hangings or wooden panels to add some warmth. All the exposed walls of the building were basic and barren with no adornment on them at all. One lonely wooden cross had been placed on a simple altar. There was a fire burning in a large hearth in the main hall that offered uncharacteristic warmth. This seemed a rare luxury in the otherwise cold building which was hundreds of years old. The feeling of age and time was not lost on Faith as she looked to the carved wooden ceiling that had withstood religious persecution of bygone eras. She stared at the fire, which fed a huge chimney.

'We keep it burning because the fire

feeds the kitchens on the other side. It is needed to keep the ovens going. We sell some of our bread and the rest is given to the workhouse in Gorbeck.' The voice came from a friendly-looking woman who had entered the hall behind her. Faith did not understand how the fire and ovens worked. The scale of the building was so great compared to her cosy home.

The short, portly nun approached, smiling at her as she neared. 'Miss, if you don't mind, you are to come with me and I shall attend to your injury.'

'And if I do mind . . . what then?' Faith asked, her manner quite curt.

'That would not be very humble or thankful now would it?' The nun stepped back and gestured towards the door with her arm outstretched. Faith did not move. The woman shook her head, the fabric from her wimple hardly moving such was the starch within it. She led the way as Faith merely stared at her, reluctant to leave the warmth of the fire.

Faith felt uneasy. She was being ungrateful and decided she was also being rude, so followed this sprightly woman along a stone-flagged corridor and into a small room. Against the wall opposite was a cot bed hardly broad enough for a person to sleep on. Upon it were placed two blankets folded neatly. A small pillow was placed atop of them. At the other end of the bed were laid out a simple woolen shift and habit.

'I have no intention of taking Holy Orders!' Faith exclaimed, appalled at the idea of being incarcerated within the walls for life. She wanted a future to look forward to, a husband of her own choosing and her family.

The woman laughed a little then placed her hand to her mouth as if she had committed a grievous sin. She stared at the open door for a moment and then replied to Faith.

'Do not worry, child. We do not take in any waif and stray who passes by to our orders. No insult meant, you understand. It is just that we do not have worldly clothes and refinements here. Our life here is basic to our needs, not our wants.' The woman looked at her seriously. 'You don't need more than this, care and, of course, food.

Faith was so relieved that her time here was not expected to be permanent that she was far from offended. By the small window that overlooked the stream as it flowed down the forested hillside was a wooden table, upon which a jug of water and a bowl had been placed. Next to it was a folded simple piece of linen by means of a towel, and an off-cut of crudely made soap.

A small hearth had been filled with a newly lit fire. The room had not had chance to warm through. She could imagine what it would be like at night. With no furnishings, not even a clip mat under foot the place felt cold and characterless. Underneath the bed was a crudely made pot and a pair of simply made leather shoes.

'Miss, you need to undress now and clean up as we will have to be looking at where you're hurt.' The woman closed the wooden door with its arched top that fitted the carved stone door frame perfectly.

Faith was rather nervous and very embarrassed. She was not used to strangers, or staying away from her small family cottage. Although it had felt crowded to the point of being unbearable at times, it was to her like heaven at the moment. Her senses were alive there with the smell of bread baking or the stew upon the open fire coupled with the constant chatter that her mother and sisters made. Faith felt bereft and isolated in this sparse, hard environment.

'Miss . . . Are you all right?' the nun asked a little nervously.

'Yes, yes,' Faith answered reassuringly, not at all sure that she was.

'Would you like me to help you to undress, miss?' the woman offered.

Possibly a little too quickly and sharply Faith answered immediately. 'No!

I can manage on my own, thank you.'

'Very well, miss. You undress and I'll fetch some of my special salve. Make sure to wash now, the piece of soap is by the jug. Mother Ruth insists that we are clean, so scrub up well and I'll be back in a few moments.' She smiled warmly at her again.

Despite the overriding feeling of fear that rose within Faith, she forced herself to smile back. 'My name is Faith . . . Faith Berry. What is yours?

'Sister Helen.' She turned to leave, but hesitated. 'Miss, if you don't mind my giving you some sound advice. Please, don't try to leave,' the woman spoke in lowered tones, 'Mother Ruth is generous to those who need help unless they are ungrateful.' She took a step toward Faith and whispered almost inaudibly, 'There are rooms, cells we call them, that have old locks and bolts on the door. You wouldn't like to stay in one of them; they are very cold. So just accept you'll be well looked after here and obey her rules, then all will be well.' She stepped back and grinned broadly as if to reinforce her kindly intentions. 'I'll be back in a few minutes. You clean up now. You'll feel much better for it.'

She left, leaving Faith staring at the closed door pondering the woman's words and evaluating her situation. She was obviously being tested so now would not be the time to run. But as Faith undressed and washed in the cold water with the rough cloth and harsh soap she promised herself she would soon find her way out. Her father, her mother and even Daniel Dell were in some sort of danger, and they were her family. Whoever this major was he had removed her liberty and threatened the safety of her family. She was grateful to him if he had meant to help or protect her in some way — why he should, she could not second guess — but family was family. She had a duty to do and do it she would. As she looked at the bruise on her side she realized it may not be for a day or so.

6

Clara watched her mother leave her home. She shook her head as she saw her go straight to the milliner's shop. Despite being given the money, she knew her mother would try to sell the gloves and earn her precious coin. She adored her but thought her to be a loving simple soul with no common sense at all. Clara's grandmother had been a well-bred woman who took up with a farmer. The result was Flora, and things had gone from bad to worse as she in turn married beneath her — Joseph Berry, a farm labourer and womaniser who had no ambition. The day would come when Clara would have her mother living under the same roof with her. Faith would be married off to someone — a soldier perhaps, or one of Daniel's men, and the girls would be placed in a school until they, too, were old enough. This town was growing and their family was going to be important within it. A network of wives from the Berry family. Then perhaps the family's fallen rank could be partially restored to them. The only thorn in their side, who constantly spoiled her plans and ambitions, was their father.

Daniel entered the room. Clara instantly stood straight, holding her stomach in, and smiled at him warmly as he leaned casually against the door frame. He was tall, and even in his fine clothes he had a rustic edge to him that she found appealing. He looked her up and down and she knew the desire they felt for each other was mutual and passionate.

'Did you see Faith in the field this morning, Daniel?' she asked as she walked over to him.

'She was running over the field the last view I had of her.' He stepped forward and kicked the door shut with his boot behind him as he embraced his wife passionately.

'Why didn't you stop for her? She could be in trouble.' Clara frowned at him after pulling herself free of his kiss. His moody grey blue eyes looked carelessly into hers. 'No need to, my dear. Your father was close behind her. I concentrated on saving my beautiful wife instead, wondering why she should be there at all.'

'Where are they then?' Clara pulled her body away from his. She knew it annoyed him, but then that was part of their game. 'Do you think they were both taken?' Mixed emotions filled her. If their father was locked up it meant she could move quickly with her plans for her family, but she would have to be certain he was not to be released. She would not have his drunken ways in her house. Her mother would do as she was instructed and the girls would learn to be ladies as she had, but what of Faith? If her reputation was ruined, who would marry her — a farmer perhaps? Then there was the other possibility to consider . . . she, too, could be in gaol. The prospect was not to be borne.

Daniel took hold of her hand and pulled her back to him. She was spun around and he lay atop her upon the chaise lounge. He was a man who liked to be masterful and she loved him for it; enough to overlook his other less attractive traits. He was the opposite of her father. Daniel knew what he wanted and how to obtain it.

She returned his embrace and kisses with equal passion. Some moments later she was almost disappointed when he stood looking down at her with his smug expression clearly betraying the joy he found in her wanton behaviour. 'If you were not my respectful wife, you'd be my first class whore!'

Clara laughed at him. 'You are too much, sir.' She stood up straightening her dress and tidying her hair in the looking glass above the fireplace. Her cheeks were very flushed.

He wrapped his arms around her waist. 'I love you, Clara Dell. You came from a hovel but if there was ever a pedigree born of mongrels, it is you.'

'So long as you appreciate that, Daniel, then we shall be happy in the extreme. I need to find out where our Faith and Father are. I can't have the mongrels running loose!' She turned around in his arms and he nodded his agreement.

'Your father fell out of the inn minutes since and I spoke to him. He said he did not see Faith. So, I don't know where she is, which is disturbing. I can hardly walk into the barracks and ask if anyone saw her there, now can I?' He released her from his embrace. 'What do I do, Clara?'

Clara thought for a moment. 'Follow Ma to the cottage. Make sure her and the girls are safe. Then find Pa. If he's drunk, dip him in the river and sober him up. Tell him one of his daughters has gone missing. I'll see if I can find out anything from the gossip in the village. Failing that, I'll have to visit Caleb myself.'

'No! I forbid it. You don't go anywhere near that man!' Now it was Daniel's face that was flushed.

'Daniel,' she smiled and kissed his bristly chin lightly. 'You're jealous. It suits you. But you have to place that behind you. I'm yours, Daniel, not his and will never be again. You know that, you took me from under his very nose, like he bought the inn from under yours, but I have to find Faith. He may know something about all this.' She kissed his neck tenderly.

'Kingsby might be behind it all. He's a meddling fool and the sooner he falls off that horse of his, the better it will be for us. He's making enemies, I tell you!' Daniel almost spat the words out.

'You sort out Father, Daniel, and I'll deal with Caleb.' She kissed him full on the mouth and he, as always, responded and agreed to fulfil her wishes.

She watched him leave. He was so strong, a pillar of the community. A man with some power and a mean streak in business yet, to her, he was a puppet who she could play with and control. Unlike the bastard, Kingsby. He was a much colder proposition. She had not broken through the man's defenses. However, pride aside, she needed him, so she summoned her maid to fetch her muffler, hat and coat. She sighed deeply, contentedly, because Clara loved her life. The pedigree then left the kennel.

* * *

Caleb had received the full report on the incident of the morning. He stared at the piece of paper from his pocket. He had taken a huge gamble by leaving it in his pocket. The man, Berry had surprised him. From his vantage point atop the coach overlooking the field he had seen the man run over his own daughter without looking back to help her. What a spineless creature who had fathered such a woman as Faith Berry. She was brave and loyal and she was a woman despite her simple girl-like clothing. He had seen that, even in her grubby, trodden state, as he had lifted her onto his horse. Caleb had noted her natural beauty. It was not as classical as her sister, Clara's, but Caleb preferred the understated subtle beauty that emanated from within. She had not hesitated from running across the fields to warn those people. He shook his head. Why on earth was he thinking about a chit of a woman from a poor family whose father was a blackguard and whose sister was . . . well he already knew that. He must be feeling under the weather or sickening for something.

Caleb stood up and stared out of his office window at the front drive of the hall. The old stables at Kemble Park now were full once more with good horses, and a new block had been built for his militia to be barracked. He would establish and keep order in this area. It was time that the villains were controlled and fairness ensued. Most of the men he had handpicked from the ranks on their return home. Grateful that someone wanted to use their skills, they were loyal to him. But he had discovered that very morning a few were still bad. He had given precise orders that no civilians were to be cut down or hurt. It had nearly turned into a fiasco, but his loyal friend and sergeant had taken them to task. It would never happen again, but he had to find the men who were spreading trouble with their poisonous words then running like frightened rabbits at the first sign of trouble. They were cowards who were paid to undermine local industry. They caused chaos, bankrupted decent, specified businesses and then the money men behind them stepped in, bought them out at low profit, and amazingly, no more trouble occurred. However, the conditions of the work force never improved. Only Caleb had, with his own money, stepped in and started to purchase them first. It was not without risk but he would survive it. He had to find Simeon Huthwaite to destroy the racket.

However, the local gentry had the

wrong idea of his dream. They wanted a corrupt system by insisting they arrest the poor man for the rich man's sins. That Caleb would never do.

He was about to return to his desk when he saw Clara approaching the gates to the hall. Driving her own gig, she was a fine figure to behold. He had been fooled by that at one time not so long ago but now he only saw trouble approaching. He stood back so that she could not see him looking at her. He had no wish to encourage her to think that Caleb Kingsby held a flicker of desire for her still. He'd met her sort before. Admittedly, they were usually of higher breeding and had learned their skills between the finest sheets in London, but in essence her kind of woman was all the same. He sat back down and played with a small knife in his fingers until the knock sounded on his office door to announce the arrival of more trouble.

7

Faith closed her eyes whilst the woman wrapped a poultice of sorts around her bruised ribs. She felt vulnerable, yet grateful that she was being tended to kindly.

'You are a lucky woman indeed. It could so easily have been broken ribs that I was trying to put back together. That is no easy task, Faith, because they can do all manner of damage to your insides. You must be strong to get away with just a bruise. Did you see who it was that stumbled over you?'

'No, I've no idea who it was. I thought it to be a horse.' Faith could see Sister Helen looking a little uneasy.

'Well, that is not right, for sure a hoof would have crushed you. Perhaps it is just as well you were unaware of who it was. There is no use harbouring grudges in this world. The good Lord spared you a bad injury.'

'I presume it was one of the Major's soldiers then,' Faith added and watched Sister Helen avert her eyes as if she knew something of it, yet did not want to say what.

Helen looked at her with a surprised expression. 'Oh no, the Major would never allow that, Faith.'

'You weren't there, were you? You have no idea what they intended to do. I heard the men in the coach talking to one another and I saw the soldiers approaching. The Major is a man of the world, Helen. The side of his character he will show to nuns is not the same as the one displayed to his men, or the common man.' Faith was quite sure of her words but Sister Helen put her arms up to protest immediately.

'You misunderstand him, Faith. You have not appreciated the man at all.' She folded her arms in front of her. 'Listen, Faith,' again she lowered her voice and spoke quietly to her, 'Major Kingsby is a man of the people. He worked hard to attain his rank. He wants fairness, he would not let the 'common man' as you describe them be trampled underfoot, especially a 'common woman'!' Although, Faith, you do not speak as if you are very common to me.' Sister Helen's face was quite flushed.

'Why are you so sure of him?' Faith asked, humbled by the woman's outspoken defense.

'Because I know him, and I'd trust him with my life. But you, miss, should be grateful that he stopped to help you. There are those who should have but who didn't.' She relaxed her stance, and smiled once more. 'I think that once the bruising has gone down, in a day or four, then you'll be well on the mend. In the meantime you will wear that wrap and I shall change it daily. You'll be amazed what Helen can do!' She blushed. 'With God's blessing, of course,' she added shyly.

'Thank you,' Faith said genuinely, as

she slipped the oversized habit over her head.

The two women looked at each other and although it hurt her side to, Faith laughed, because the garment swamped her, but with Helen's help and her belt they managed to make it wearable.

'Mother Ruth wishes to see you, Faith, after prayers.' She pondered for a moment then added, 'Just answer her questions simply and please don't argue with her. Don't say anything bad against Caleb Kingsby or you will vex her. She is a woman who expects respect.'

Her earnest countenance touched Faith. She wondered what this Mother Ruth had done to her in the past, and why. After all, Helen seemed the most gentle of creatures.

'Can we go for a walk around the abbey grounds, Helen?' Faith asked looking optimistically at her.

'Well . . . I . . . Perhaps I should ask Mother Ruth first . . . ' Helen looked sideways rather nervously.

'I don't intend to run away. I wouldn't do that to you.' Sister Helen looked very relieved so Faith felt compelled to add, 'Not when you are with me because I don't want you to be held responsible for my actions,' hoping she was not betraying her intentions too soon.

'Faith, I am always responsible for you. It is I who had you placed in the comfortable cells as a guest. If you run away it is I who will serve the penance for my misjudgement of you.' Sister Helen was most serious.

Faith's smile dropped from her face. 'That is so unfair!' Then she corrected herself. 'No, it is clever, because she is using you to control me.' She placed her hand on Helen's shoulder. 'It is just as well you are a good judge of character and that I have a conscience.'

It was Helen's turn to smile. 'Come on then. You can see Mother Ruth and then I'll show you the gardens, but we'll be called for prayers in about an hour.'

'We?' Faith repeated the word,

wondering what that would be like. Her prayers to God were like little informal chats. Well, she did the chatting, but sometimes things worked out like she'd asked. Other times they didn't, but then there would be a reason so, she reasoned most of the time. Formal prayers sounded much more daunting. In church, yes, where there are other sinners, normal folk, but in the company of devout nuns, well it just seemed very daunting to her.

'Yes, 'we'. You have to kneel and do as I do. Just stay quiet and remember to look humble. You never know, you might like the experience. God chooses us at different stages of our lives.'

'Should we walk?' Faith asked, wanting to feel the fresh air on her face once more and change the subject. She saw Sister Helen shake her head at her. However, Faith felt much better when she was led out of the tiny room. This lady, Mother Ruth, was a clever woman who Faith had no wish to meet.

* ★ *

The light tapping sound on the door told Caleb his uninvited guest had arrived.

'Enter,' he said boldly, and placed the knife down on the desk in front of him. Then thought better of it and slipped it back into his pocket.

The door was swung wide open as Clara swept into the room with her head held high, her smile bright and her eyes positively shining as they focussed upon Caleb's relaxed form. He rose to his feet, greeted her like a long term friend, which in a way she had been, once. Then without further comment both seated themselves at opposing sides of his desk. Caleb waited for her to explain her unannounced arrival.

'Caleb, I must ask you to excuse my rather bold visit.' Her mouth dramatically changed to a very serious expression. 'Frankly, I need your help . . . Caleb.' She flushed delicately as she uttered his name softly, looking at him with wide puppy-dog eyes.

'Are you in some sort of trouble, Clara? Can Dell not pay his tavern bill?'

She ignored this jibe at her husband's habits.

'Nothing like that! It is about Faith, Caleb,' she said simply.

'Then perhaps you need to go to church,' Caleb replied sarcastically. This time he noted a glint of anger in her eyes.

'Caleb, you are not making this easy for me. I find your manner extremely offensive.'

'Did you really expect it to be any other, Clara?' He stared at her defiantly.

'I can't find my sister, Faith, anywhere, Caleb and I wondered if you had seen her or knew of her where-abouts.' Clara ignored his protest; instead she quivered her bottom lip a little as she spoke to him hoping he would soften his manner.

'Why should I have seen her, Clara? I tend to stay well away from you and your family.' He saw how his words had annoyed her but she did well to restrain herself.

'You have no need to, Caleb. My family are completely unaware that you acted in any way less than a gentleman toward me. In fact, I can go further to state they have no knowledge of a connection between us at all.' She stared directly into his eyes. 'I prefer it that way. I am respectably married now.'

'Respectable? You were not so when you willingly lay in my arms, or have you forgotten those days so easily?' He raised a quizzical brow, then added dismissively, 'Is your father not out there looking for her?'

Caleb was watching her calculating eyes as they flickered like candle lights showing a spectrum of emotions.

'There was a disturbance this morning, over at the Clitheroe's field. I fear that as she made her way to the village to meet with my mother and father, she may have inadvertently become caught up in it. Can you not put my mind at rest and assure me that she was not injured in any way or locked up by your soldiers?'

'Where is your father, Clara?' Caleb watched her lower her lids slightly. She knew that little girl lost look was attractive, it brought back memories of how easily he once fell under her spell.

'I don't know at the moment. I suspect he is trying to find Faith. Daniel is looking for them both. But Father was seen at the inn.' She looked up at him. 'So can I presume that Faith was not arrested, then?' she persisted.

Caleb stood up, and walked around to her. He leaned on the desk in front of her. 'Faith Berry is not in the cells.'

He was at least pleased to see the flicker of relief in her eyes. His close proximity to her brought an unexpected reaction from the now respectably married woman. She rubbed the back of her gloved hand against his leg gently.

He placed it between his hands. 'You are a very sensuous lady, Clara. Tell me, why did you really come here? Does your concern really reach out as far as your sister?'

'Caleb!' She pulled her hand away from his. 'There was a time when you thought good of me. As I remember it you would not flinch from my touch or doubt my sincerity.' She looked up at him, this time her pretence was cast aside. 'I needed to see you.'

'That was before I walked in on you and Dell!' He returned to his chair and leaned on the desk almost glaring at her.

'You never did let me explain, Caleb.' Now it was her turn to lean forwards. 'How could I placate you and put things right between us when you wouldn't let me within ten paces of you. What you saw was nothing . . . it meant nothing. He forced me into an embrace. I had not offered it and would never have done so willingly. We were happy! You treated me like a lady.' Her words were spoken softly.

'Neither did you pull away from him.

I liked you as my lover, Clara. As I recall I was not your first. A lady, Clara, I would have married. You made your bed, 'lady', mine no longer is open to you, so go and sleep with Dell.' She raised a hand to strike his face but he grasped her wrist with sufficient strength to stop it in its path. 'Tell him that if I catch him and his friends causing trouble in this area again he'll hang alongside them. Good day, Clara.' He released his grip and turned away from her, staring out of the window.

'What do you mean . . . 'his friends'? He is a business man, he knows lots of people!' Clara ran to him. She was infuriated that he would speak so boldly to her and in such a detached manner. Hadn't he been her lover and shared so much with her, happily — at least for a time.

'He'll know what I mean and if you don't, then I strongly suggest that you ask him what he was doing on the field. Mind, what the hell he was doing letting you be caught up in it defies even my low opinion of him.' His face was stern as he stared at her.

'I was going to meet Ma and Faith. I only stopped there out of curiosity. I had no idea what was occurring there. I thought the man was one of the Bible Moth preachers.' She placed her hand on his arm. 'Caleb, you must believe me.'

'No, ma'am, I must not. You see, I once did and you played me false. So please go to your man and deliver my message, for I have no wish to see you on the streets.'

Clara let her arm drop, her face paled. 'I'm so sorry you feel that way, Caleb, truly I am.' She seemed dispirited as she left. Caleb grabbed his coat and hat. He felt tainted by the whole affair, his and Clara's and her bloody father's conniving ways. He would have to return to Faith Berry shortly with news of what was left of her family, a thought that brought him no pleasure at all for she deserved better in his eyes.

8

Faith waited on a stone bench under a plain archway outside Mother Ruth's office, hoping to be called for her first meeting. She had decided to arrive early rather than risk the infamous woman's wrath. However, her knock had remained unanswered, so she had sat down and waited patiently until the cold seeped from the stone into her body then she had thought better of it. She looked along the cloisters; the open quadrangle was sparse like the abbey itself. The few plants that grew in the central garden gave the harsh stone its only softness by nature of the contrast to its solid form. Faith decided she had time to walk around it under the shadow of the arches to pass some time.

She could not help thinking about her own mother, and her sisters Sarah and Jane. What must they be feeling about her absence? Would they be pining for her or was her absence explained and accepted? Somehow, she would break free from this Holy place, her prison. However, Faith was also very aware how any misdemeanor she created would be laid at Sister Helen's feet. Faith wished she did not like the woman so much. Her bruising was now healing as the poultices seemed to have absorbed all the sharp pains, leaving her only with gentler aches. She knew her feelings for the woman were more than mere gratitude, though, because she found Helen refreshing, educated and willing to share her knowledge with her new friend and pupil. Faith walked slowly around in the shadows looking up at the carved stone gargoyles which appeared at intervals, grinning hideously down on those who passed by.

It was as she was standing still staring at one of these that she saw someone move in the corner ahead of her. They had just descended a spiral staircase and entered the cloister. Swiftly, Faith leaned against the wall behind one of the columns which graced the side of the doors to the abbey itself. Why she behaved so, she did not really understand, because all she was doing was walking around a cloister. However, her every action had to have the permission of Mother Ruth, via Sister Helen, and as she had not sought permission to walk around the cloister, she stayed incognito, hoping her presence would not be known.

The other nuns never engaged in conversation with her. It was as if because she was from the outside world, she carried a risk of spreading some strange contagion from her world into their minds. So, by and large, she remained ignored. This suited Faith for it gave her time to assess the abbey's layout, where she could go unseen and where she could not.

'Ruth, you are so kind to risk all and hide us here.' The gruff voice was no more than a whisper, but Faith was near enough to hear the words as they drifted over cold stone on the still air. There was something about the man's inflection that was strangely familiar to her.

'Simeon, you test my patience to the limit. I cannot have you using my Abbey as a safe house. You dabble dangerously in the affairs of man whilst I am trying to run a house of God!' Her message was sharp yet her words were spoken no louder than his. 'You were very nearly seen arriving here this time,' she added. 'Your men were almost caught by the militia. Think of it, the scandal if you were arrested outside the abbey! Do you know a man nearly died as a result of the furore you caused? Does that not bother you? Will you stop this madness now before it is the end of you and all concerned. You do not need all this power. What for, Simeon? Life is better when all is simple. The more you have the more you want and for what? You chase the devil's goals!' Her voice rose slightly.

'By whom was I nearly seen? You can

tell your women to keep their silence,' he chuckled, 'I've seen the iron rod you wield over them. If they only knew your brother was a wanted man! Accused, suspected, yet no one can tie me in to the 'troubles', and they won't because soon the damage will be complete and I will have what I desire. So you run your house and soon I shall have my own to run. Kemble Park will belong to the Huthwaites as it always should have done.'

'Simeon, Kingsby was here. He nearly saw you. I'd only just ushered in your louts when he arrived.' Mother Ruth's voice was so quiet again it was hardly audible. 'I tell you, your aims and methods are not honorable. Do not come here any more, Simeon. My conscience is troubling me, even if you have none!' She took a step back but a man's hand grabbed her arm and pulled her back to the stairwell.

'You will not tell me what to do, my Ruth. You will obey me as your elder brother. I will tell you when I no longer need these rooms but for now you will carry on fulfilling your duties and if that insect Kingsby should pass by here again you will send him on his way. This is a house for women, not him. So why was he here, anyway?' His question made Faith hold her breath for she had no wish to be brought in to their affairs, whatever they were, they were not of God and Mother Ruth knew that it was so.

'He . . . he calls this way occasionally. He is a man of faith.' Mother Ruth had covered for her. Why?

'Then tell him to go to his own church but do not encourage him to enter here. When we have bought up what is left of the mill and the mine he shall be glad of your solace. Believe me, Ruth, if his men catch Gibbons before our work is done he will need your prayers. I will destroy him before he can me. Until then keep him outside your strong medieval doors.'

Faith heard feet running up the stairs again and then a door slammed shut.

Ruth walked briskly around the other side of the cloisters, returning to her office. Faith stayed where she was until she knew that Ruth was safely inside. Then she made her way around to the door and knocked gently upon it.

A moment later she heard the voice she had previously dreaded but now almost pitied. Here was a woman torn between her faith, her duty and her family. Suddenly Faith realised that what she was feeling towards her was empathy for a woman she had not yet met.

'Enter!' The woman's voice was sharp and loud.

Faith walked into the large room which was sparse except for her desk, chair, Bible and cross. 'Faith Berry, ma'am,' she said deciding that would explain enough as to why she was there.

The woman stood up and walked over to her.

'So you are the scrap of a girl who has caused so much trouble!' Ruth's stare was piercing as she looked down into Faith's eyes.

'I am unaware of causing anyone any 'trouble', Ma'am.' Faith stared straight back into the woman's slightly blood-shot eyes.

'You have an insolent manner about you. Lose it, girl, if you want to see the kindly side of my nature. I do not approve of such disrespectful behaviour. I understand you caused a stampede amongst the villagers in which you yourself were injured.' She folded her arms across her body whilst continuing to stare at Faith.

'No, I warned the good speakers that they risked arrest by the militia if they stayed. It was the men who overheard my words who panicked the workers. I merely hoped the speaker would ask them to calmly disperse, yet they did not.' Faith was very calm. Ruth appeared more agitated by this unexpected confidence which Faith displayed.

'Yet, you are brought here by the very leader of the same militia whom you warned them against. How split your loyalties must be.' Ruth's face was slightly flushed.

'No, ma'am, they are not. However, my heart grieves for those who are. I acted at the time as I thought was right. I did not understand perhaps, the gravity of the situation. I am grateful to Major Kingsby for bringing me safely here and I hope to be able to utter my thanks to him at some point in the future. I would like to thank you for the care that Sister Helen has shown me. I fear without it I could have been in a deal of pain still. I hope that one day I will be able to repay you for this.' Faith saw the woman take a step back, still looking at her, sizing her up. The inner turmoil was almost visible in her eyes.

'Tell me, child, what do you understand now?' Ruth asked her.

Faith was careful in how she answered because if she put a word wrong the cell with the lock and bolt beckoned. 'I understand that I should keep away from the matters of men and focus on my family. My mother must be very concerned for my safety as will my sisters be.'

'I am sure that Major Kingsby has sent word to them.' Ruth took hold of her hand and led her to the window that looked out across the stream and woods.

'This is a beautiful place is it not?' she asked quietly, her eyes almost looked moist with emotion.

'Yes, it is. It is peaceful and God has blessed the Abbey with good soil for the food you grow.' Faith watched the woman's expression change, soften as she obviously agreed with her words.

Ruth spun around, as if suddenly aware of Faith's closeness. She leaned against the stone wall. 'Girl, how did you know the militia were to be sent there?'

'I heard the man in the coach say so,' Faith answered honestly.

'Do you make it a habit to eavesdrop on other people's conversations?' Ruth was staring at her almost knowingly. This time it was Faith who blushed slightly.

'No, but sometimes you can't help it. God puts us in places by chance on occasion and then we must act upon it. Last time I acted without thinking . . . impulsively, and it was nearly my downfall.' Faith watched a smile form upon the woman's lips.

'And this time? What do you intend to do with your latest blessing from our Lord?' Ruth held her hands loosely in front of her as if steadying her own nerves.

'This time?' Faith repeated trying to look innocent.

'You would not have entered here so promptly, so confidently and so emphatically if you had not been privy to my personal conversation out there.' Faith looked out of the window nervously. 'So what do you intend to do with the information you have gleaned?' Ruth persisted.

'I cannot 'do' anything, Ma'am, for Sister Helen is responsible for my behaviour as well as my safe-keeping and I would not see her harmed in any way. She is my friend.' Faith looked back at her, searching for a mutual understanding between them. She could help Ruth, if the woman would trust in her to do so. But would she?

Faith saw the smile broaden and relief shine through her eyes.

'Good, you are a sensible woman. You may go back to your friend but I will speak to you again, Faith Berry, and then you will listen to my words carefully.'

She stared out of the window and Faith left the room, grateful that she had thus survived her first trial with Mother Ruth.

9

Caleb needed to find a connection between Gibbons and Simeon, then he could prove that the man was behind all the troubles caused. One of the machines at the mills had been wrecked by a stirred mob three days since. The irony was that the local mill workers had quite good conditions. These were men using workers' genuine complaints in surrounding counties to gain their own ambitions.

Every time he got anywhere near him they were blocked; it was like trying to grab hold of a slippery eel. He would find the weakest link in their chain and break it. The man he sought was seduced by drink — Joseph Berry. He had not been seen at the Falcon Inn since Dell chased him out of there. The one-time local watering hole for the local villains was now a respectable coaching inn but occasionally Joseph returned to his old haunt. So where was he now?

Caleb rode out to the small cottage that Berry shared with his wife and daughters. He thought about bringing his men but had decided that they would be too easily seen. So instead he took the old path through the forest with his sergeant covering his back, a man he had worked with for years, whom he trusted with his life. He still hoped that his and Dell's path would not cross along the way. Their lives had crossed twice before; the first time was in the army, when Caleb had had him flogged for stealing supplies. He was lucky not to have been hung. Wellington had had men strung up for stealing a chicken from their Spanish allies before. Dell had been far from grateful though, and now Caleb wondered if he should have taken the man's life after all. It was not what he believed in, unless to protect himself or in the fight against another army. To string up one of his own men would have bothered his conscience deeply. Now, it appeared he was paying the price for his weakness, or his conscience.

Dell had wanted revenge and once he found the opportunity he had also found it exceedingly sweet. His chance had come here, in their own country, back in their own village. Dell had seduced Caleb's woman. Unknown to the both of them, Caleb had no intention of marrying her. She was a young, pretty woman who wanted to improve her lot, which had suited Caleb at first. Then he tired of her manipulative ways and hankered for something more lasting, and more genuine. How, though, to find her a position which appeased her but did not involve him?

Caleb had decided to form the local militia. It had been a project that kept his days busy for long hours, recruiting men that would otherwise be without work. It was a project that took him away from his home. So Dell moved in on Clara and unwittingly solved a problem for her lover. Dell had not realised that or he would never have married her. Instead, Caleb let them believe he had lost the love of his life, and whilst Dell celebrated by taking his wife to Harrogate after the wedding, Caleb had bought out the Falcon Inn from under Dell's nose. The vendetta had begun. Now they hated each other openly. They each had purchased part of the village and each sought to outgrow the other in power — Caleb to protect it from the likes of Dell, and the latter to control it, the trade through it and gain influence. Caleb had the newly-formed militia, backed by the local gentry; he purchased Kemble Park along with the inn and the stables. Dell had acquired two houses, the cooper's, and was trying to buy the baker's and set up a forge. He was raising money by methods unknown but Caleb guessed the funds were partly in payment for making arrangements and deals on behalf of Huthwaite, whose own goals were to own both the mill and the mines.

Caleb was tired of the deceptions and the charades that the men played; himself included to a point. He wanted to settle this and be free to focus on his business and build a better life. He wanted a family of his own, a woman who he could trust, but he would only fulfil this ambition when all the feuding was done with.

He approached the cottage, walking the horse casually toward it, and waited to see if the door was opened. He wondered who, if anyone, would greet him. He glanced to his left and instinctively knew where James had stopped in the trees. The door opened and Flora Berry ran out.

She stopped a few feet from his side. She was rubbing her hands in her apron. 'Oh, Major, I'm so pleased to see you. I'd ask you in but I'm in the middle of . . . of . . . preparing some skins.' She hesitated momentarily then added rather abruptly, 'I have lost my

daughter, Faith. Can you find her, sir?'
She was almost shaking and his heart
was filled with guilt because he had
thought the family to be a selfish and
uncaring one.

'I understand she is fine and being
taken good care of. I am sure she will
return to you soon. Is your husband at
home, Mrs Berry? I should like a word
with him.' He saw the pain in the
woman's face and could see a similarity
between her and the daughter, Faith.

He watched as she looked nervously
around her, glancing back to the
cottage. 'No, he isn't able to speak to
you today.' She looked relieved as if she
had hidden her lie well within a
modicum of truth. 'Can I give him a
message for you, sir?'

'Yes, tell him that Caleb Kingsby
wants to speak to him . . . and soon.'

She took a step toward the horse and
stroked its neck, still resembling a
frightened rabbit, but she had found the
courage to look up into his face. 'I will
be sure to tell him,' she said in a clear

voice. Then added in a whisper, 'If you see my Faith will you tell her I love and miss her and please keep her safe for me.' Her eyes watered as she spoke.

He leaned forward; he, too, stroked the animal's neck. 'I will, but perhaps it is you who should come and talk to me?' He raised an eyebrow before sitting up straight. 'Tell him, Mrs Berry.' He nodded to her, then turned the horse around and rode off, surprised that the woman who had a reputation for being weak and muddle-brained showed a glimmer of sharp wit. Perhaps his answers would come from the Berry family after all — not from the whore or the drunkard, but from a devotedly loyal mother. The ways of the world amazed him. He wondered if it was time to speak to Faith again. She may not even realise that she too had knowledge he needed.

10

Faith approached the door to the outside world with mixed feelings. She wanted to walk beyond the gardens and across the fields to go home. It was the sense of freedom that opening the doors gave her. It was now two days since Mother Ruth had spoken to her. Since then she had been given time to walk on her own as if a silent trust had formed between the two. She had spoken to her one further time. It was a cryptic conversation that left her wondering what the woman meant. She had said that she would leave her to choose her own path and to her own conscience to discern what that path should be. Her own, she said, was already set. Sister Helen was no longer her constant companion. Today she had been sent to collect herbs and tend to a few chores in the garden.

She loved the place for it was down near the stream. It was peaceful and clean. After stretching the time it took to fulfil her chores for as far as she dared, she looked up from her squat position, as a shadow fell upon her.

'You look as if the life suits you here,' Caleb spoke to her and squatted down opposite. 'I have a message for you. Your mother says she loves and misses you very much.'

'Thank you for telling me, sir. Can I go to her now, or is my imprisonment not completed?' Faith looked at him. She wanted to be angry with him but she found it was not a sincere emotion. He had brought her to safety and now delivered greetings from her mother, words she had longed to hear from the woman herself.

'I would ask you to stay a few more days. I have no power to keep you here but I have reason to believe you will be safer at the abbey until I fulfil my current duties.' He broke off a piece of grass and played with it in his fingers.

Faith glanced up to Ruth's window, remembering the men and the conversation she had had with her. Caleb had brought her here to protect her, yet he was now in grave danger. 'Let us go into the shelter of the abbey.' She stood up wanting to lead him to a secluded place away from where Ruth or the men could see him if they glanced out of their windows.

'Walk me to the cloisters, then, because I need to speak with Mother Ruth,' he said to her casually.

'No! Not there. Wait in the main hall and I'll tell her you are here.' Faith had overreacted to his suggestion. Suspicion instantly clouded his face.

'Why not the cloisters, Faith?' he asked straight away.

'Because they . . . are being used right now . . . for prayers.' Faith linked her arm around his and led him toward the front of the abbey.

'Strange, because I did not hear anyone speaking as I walked past them just now.' He did not believe her at all, that was obvious.

'No one has stated that prayers have to be said out loud, sir,' she answered quickly.

Once they were at the side of the abbey where they could not be overlooked or overheard, he stopped her and stood in front, blocking her path. 'Have I been blind, Faith? Am I combing the area looking for something which is under my very nose? Is there someone here who I want to see? Have they claimed sanctuary . . . your father, for instance?'

'Major Kingsby, my father is not here, not that I know of anyway, but you . . . you should leave here. Let me go with you. It is time I went home to see, Ma. Clara must be beside herself with worry over me . . . ' Faith began to speak but his cynical laugh surprised her.

'Clara will be absolutely fine, believe me.' He placed a hand on her shoulder. 'You are so very different, Faith.'

'You speak as if you know her well,

Major. How so?' Faith watched him divert his gaze.

'If I speak honestly to you, Faith, honestly mind, even if you find the truth unpalatable, will you do me the honour in return, by telling me who is hiding here and why? For then I can set a trap to catch them without endangering anyone in the abbey.' He stared into her eyes and she knew in her heart that this was a man she could trust.

'Yes, but you must tell me what secret you hide concerning my sister, first.'

He nodded. 'Faith Berry, I have every respect for you and your mother. However, you will lose what little respect you have for me for I would have you know the truth of it. Your sister and I were lovers of convenience for a few months prior to her wedding. I am sorry if that shocks you but it is the truth. She is a resourceful woman who wanted to attain a position in the village by any means she could. We were happy with each other but not in love.

However, Dell thinks he won her from me . . . ' His voice trailed away and he dropped his hand from her shoulder. 'I understand if you think bad of me but now please be honest with me. Tell me what you have found here other than nuns.'

Faith was strangely resigned to the fact that her sister had been far more 'worldly' than her. She had seen her and Daniel running into the woods together, a look of eagerness upon their faces. 'No, I believe you tell me the truth.' She blushed slightly, 'I can only apologise for my sister's lack of propriety. However, my mother must never know. We are very different people, sir.'

'Now, explain about the cloisters, Faith.'

'Simeon someone and a man called Gibbons were in the tower room two days since. I do not know if they are still there but Ruth is in a terrible position. She wants them to leave the abbey but this Simeon is her brother. I think she is torn in loyalty and fear. Can you help her?' Faith was most anxious that Caleb did not burst in and search the rooms on his own. She grabbed hold of his sleeve. 'I know you are a soldier but I ask you to leave now. Have the abbey watched if you need to but do not enter the building on your own.'

He smiled at her. 'After what I have just told you I am flattered that you care enough to stop me, Faith.' He was standing so close to her she could feel his breath brush her cheek. Both had not wanted to be overheard, but neither had realised how close they had become.

'You did not force yourself on her, Caleb. If I know my sister well enough she will have found a way of making you aware of her first.' Faith looked into his deep brown eyes and saw that he was quite surprised by her reaction. 'Caleb, she was born a flirt. That is not an excuse but it is the truth of it. Ma could only see beauty, not menace.'

'Faith, go inside and change into your normal clothes. I'm taking you away from here. I'll wait for you by the road. Come as soon as you can.' He kissed her cheek very lightly. 'I want you safe. You are too naïve to be left in a building with such rogues, but you have helped me in my mission tremendously. You shall not be involved further.' He ran along the side of the abbey and then into the adjacent woods.

Faith waited for a moment before entering the abbey. Her face was flushed from the concern he showed for her safety, and one thought dominated her mind . . . how could Clara have been so stupid as to let a man like that slip through her fingers and instead take up with the likes of Daniel Dell?

11

Sister Helen stood next to her elder sister, The Abbess, Ruth, as they gazed down upon Faith and Caleb in the garden. They stood in silence until both of them moved away from the garden and out of sight.

'They look so good together. Do you think she will tell him, Ruth?' Helen asked anxiously.

'Oh, yes, I am certain of it.' Ruth looked at her young sister and patted her shoulder affectionately.

'How can you be so sure?' Helen looked up emotionally. 'She might try to protect you like she tried to protect me when she thought you would punish me.' Helen smiled a little for they had, by their own connivance, proved Faith to be an honourable person by the way she had stood by her word to Helen.

'She will tell him for the very same

reason, to protect us all. She under-stands what it is to be torn by conscience, between what is right and one's loyalty to one's own family. Let her leave with a peaceful heart, Helen. Go to her, tell her that I release her.' Ruth sat down at her table looking extremely tired.

'Ruth, if Simeon has done wrong things, he will be punished. Our family . . . ' her voice trailed off.

'We have no family other than our Holy Father, and our fellow sisters here. All else is not of our world. Not anymore. We can not ignore or condone his actions . . . particularly if they involve people being hurt. Be strong, Helen, and have faith that all will be well. Wrongs will be righted.'

★   ★   ★

Faith removed the now familiar uni-form replacing it with her old dress. It had been cleaned and felt new again; or at least, newer. She brushed out her hair and was about to tie it back with her piece of ribbon when the door opened slowly behind her. She would not even have seen it if she had not been flicking her dark blonde hair out. It was a liberating feeling after the constraints of her habit and wimple.

She froze mid stroke of the brush as she saw the figure of her father standing in the doorway staring back at her.

'You know it is a funny thing, lass. You can live with someone and not even realise how much they've grown up. Your ma's right, you're more than ready for a man. So tell me what you're doing cooped up in a nun house?' He stepped inside and leaned against the wall nonchalantly.

To Faith he looked dirty, grubby and ill-befitting his surroundings. They rarely held conversation. He told her to do chores occasionally but, on the few occasions he was at the cottage, much time was spent nagging her poor mother or sleeping off his excesses.

'What are you doing here, Pa? Does

Mother Ruth know that there is a man in the building?' Faith asked him and saw the familiar sneer cross his face. Faith prayed that bad blood did not really run in families because, if it was so, she would prefer to remain childless.

'Why are you here?' His voice was sharp. She knew if she did not answer him, the next thing he would do would be to throw the chair at the wall or some such action. He was a bully and she realised, God forgive her, how much she hated him.

'I was brought here when I was injured on the field. We were listening to the man speak and the crowd went wild when the soldiers turned up. I was pushed to the ground by someone. The nuns have helped me to recover from the knock I received.' Faith quickly tied her hair back.

'I should have known when he described the wench who warned him, that it was my own daughter. Can you believe it? You saved your Pa from being arrested. You should be proud, lass.' He walked over to the cot and picked up the habit with one hand. 'You suited this. You're not like our Clara. That one knows the world. She don't have that arrogance in her eyes when she looks at her Pa, but you do. She's a good girl, did her pa's bidding.' He stared at her a moment longer as if stressing a point.

'She was more than glad to marry Daniel. She loves him.' Faith found herself defending Clara which was a new experience to her.

'Aye, that she does but it came at a price.' He flicked a hair away from her cheek. Faith recoiled. She did not want him near her.

All the time she wasted here with him, Caleb was waiting for her. How long would he wait? She desperately wanted to leave and be with him.

'Whatever the price, I know she would pay it gladly to be with a man she loves,' Faith said. 'I must say my goodbyes now to Sister Helen and go and see Ma. She'll be fretting about me.' Faith picked up her bonnet.

'What about your friend Caleb Kingsby? Isn't he waiting for yer some where?' He grinned at her almost mockingly.

'Major Kingsby brought me here because I was injured. I shall, in time, pay my respects to the man and thank him, but Ma is my first priority.'

'Your sister paid him enough respects and told me all about his plans as they unfurled. You don't need to. You'll be found a husband for you and then you'll be out of harm's way and grateful to your Pa for doing so.'

Faith's eyes were wide, her mouth dropped open as the force of his words hit her. 'You knew that Clara and Kingsby were lovers, yet you did nothing to stop them or insist upon them marrying?'

'I instigated it. Mind, Dell interfering as he did was a right blessing. Aye, she's a resourceful lass, our Clara. You go to your Ma and I'll see you there later. Mind you don't get lost upon the way, though, or I'll not be happy with Ma that she has bred such feckless women. Stay away from Kingsby, he won't be around much longer so don't go getting all pally with him, his day's done. You tell Ma to keep the girls and herself in the cottage tomorrow. Not to go visiting Clara. There'll be trouble around and I want you all out of it.'

Faith tried to walk past him but he gripped her arm tightly. 'You open that sweet mouth of yours one more time and interfere in the affairs of men and I'll see it is shut firmly. I'll find you a husband at the next market day. You'll go to the highest bidder. You understand me, girl?'

She glanced down at his hand then looked straight into his eyes. 'Yes, I understand you, Father.'

He released his hold on her. 'Good, now you be sure to go straight home and that way you keep Ma safe and well.'

Faith walked out of the cell feeling almost sick to her stomach. These men preyed on blackmailing their own families. They were bullies and she hated them. She crossed the main hall to the abbey doors. She didn't look back but was aware that Sister Helen and Mother Ruth were watching her from the shadows. The women did not step forward into the open so Faith nodded slightly as she passed them by.

12

Faith ran across the fields and through the trees towards the road which she hoped would lead her to Caleb and safety. Then she would go to her mother and home. Faith was frightened but she knew what she had to do. She had to protect her mother and sisters at all costs.

She eventually stumbled out onto the road and stopped, breathing heavily. Her side had not ached so much in days. She looked along it but could not see Caleb anywhere. Her spirits sank; she thought he would have waited for her.

★ ★ ★

Simeon kicked over a stool as Joseph Berry returned to the room. 'So did you tell her?' he asked sharply, annoyance sounding clear in his voice.

Berry smiled nervously at the intimidating man in front of him. 'Aye, I did, sir. You make no worries. She'll not say a word to Kingsby. Her and her ma are like village mice, no spine to them. They'll cover for me and tell the militia what I tell them to.'

'You had better be right, man. I need you at the hall tomorrow night. Gibbons will set up another meet near the mill in the evening. This time there will be no chance for word to get to the militia. The men are ripe for trouble so we'll show them how to go about it. You, though, will go to Kemble Park. I want you to burn down the barracks — but you have to be careful, man, where you set the fires.'

'Oh, I will, sir. I knows how to set a good fire, don't you doubt it. I'll not get harmed.' Berry looked relieved that the man had showed some concern but he had misunderstood the man's intentions.

'Be careful that you don't damage the

hall — I want it unspoiled. I'm not buying a ruin. I want to buy it cheaply. The stables and the barracks can be turned to ashes but the hall has to be sound.'

Berry scratched his stubbly chin. 'What about Kingsby?' he asked, his eyes gleaming at the prospect of doing the man some permanent harm. He had used Clara but thought himself too good for her, so Berry would enjoy bringing him low.

'Make sure he's caught in the fire.' Huthwaite lowered his voice as he spoke but Berry raised his brows. 'He burns, too!'

'You want me to murder him?' Joseph Berry asked and swallowed.

'No, I want you to beat him senseless, leave him doused in brandy in his stables and then set the fire going. The smoke will do the job for you. Everyone will think he's been drinking and if a lamp was found near his grilled bones then they'd also come to thinking he'd set it himself. No suspect, the man's remains will be proof enough. No blame, no more Kingsby. I'll restore order to the area with his militia and bale out the mine. The mill will follow in time with one last resurgence of trouble from the rabble. Now are you clear about what you have to do, man?' He placed a hand on the back of Berry's neck and the man felt himself tremble, like Ma did when he did it to her.

'Yes,' he gulped and smiled up at the well groomed face next to him.

'Good.' He slapped Berry hard on the back causing him to take a step forwards. 'I'm riding back home tonight. I'll take a drink in the Peacock and Pheasant then make sure someone escorts me to my bed. That way, I can't be implicated. You take Gibbons with you. He can watch your back whilst you're busy.'

'Right, sir,' Berry answered, glad of the offer of help from another. If things didn't go right he'd slip away and make sure Gibbons was found. 'Thank you, sir.' Berry hesitated.

'Was there something else, man?' Simeon Huthwaite asked.

'I have a family to feed and wondered if there'd be a reward for this piece of work.' He saw Simeon smile and place his hand in his pocket.

'Here,' he tossed him a coin, 'Now listen, Joseph. You do this well and there'll be five fine silver coins waiting for you. But I don't want you drinking before you do it.'

'Not a drop, sir. I give you my word.' Berry left and ran down the stairs a happy man.

Gibbons entered the room after he had left. Simeon looked to him. 'You wait till he's done the job then make sure he dies whilst trying to rescue the horses. He can die a hero.'

Gibbons nodded.

'I don't want a drunkard with a loose mouth left around the village. He has become a liability. Do it cleanly, man. No errors.' He tossed him a pouch with coin in.

'Aye, sir. You can rely on me.'

★   ★   ★

Faith had only taken two steps when the horse and rider rode onto the road ahead of her. She smiled instantly, relieved that he had waited for her.

'I thought you had decided to take your vows,' he said and returned a smile as he put down his hand for her to grab and climb up behind him.

'We must leave quickly. If my father sees us we are in a deal of trouble.'

'I thought your father was not one of the men there?' he said quickly.

'Yes he is. He came to me as I gathered my things. He threatened me and Ma and you, Caleb, are in danger,' she spoke rapidly. 'Can we leave now and go somewhere I can explain, for I must not be seen with you.'

'Yes, of course.' He rode into the cover of the woods, walking the horse through the trees. Once they were safely hidden from view he helped her down, holding the horse's reins in his hand. As he lifted her down she slipped into his arms. It was as she placed her head against his chest and closed her eyes, shamed that she felt like crying, yet needing the comfort he afforded her.

He stroked her cheek with his hand. 'Tell me what it is that you feel, Faith.' He tilted her face to hers.

'Lost,' she said simply. 'I love my mother, I love my sisters and I hate my own father. I will not be his puppet but he uses them as a weapon against me. I need you to protect them and end this nightmare. Caleb . . . I need you.'

13

Clara was determined to find Faith. She had to be back home by now. Whatever it was that was going on in her family, she was going to get to the bottom of it and her plan for the future could then be put into action.

Her morning's plans were rudely interrupted when she was surprised by her father's sudden entry into the house. Had he pulled the bell cord at the front door he would have been stopped by the servant but he cared nothing for propriety so he had made his way through the back door, ignoring the woman's protests in the kitchen as he grabbed a pie in passing and continued up into the main hall of the house. Clara was just coming down the stairs when she heard the commotion.

'Father!' she exclaimed loudly and saw the servant return, flustered, to the kitchen. 'What brings you here so . . . unannounced?' She stepped down into the hallway and looked at the floor by his muddied boots. 'You're crumbing the pie, Father.' She shouted down the servants' corridor, 'Fetch a brush and a plate, girl!'

'When does a father need to be announced to his own daughter?' He stared at her defiantly.

Clara felt as though something was irritating her skin. It was the feeling that made her uncomfortable whenever the man was around her. 'Come into the morning room, Father.' She looked down at his feet. 'Please don't stand on my rugs.'

She took the plate off the girl and gave it to him then led the way into the room. It was no surprise to her that he casually dropped it on a table carelessly and shoved the rest of the pie into his mouth. He strode boldly over to the fireplace, walking across her new hearthrug, leaving his debris behind, and stared around the room grimacing but nodding at the surroundings he envied, yet admired.

'What do you want?' she asked curtly.

'You've done grand, lass. See I told you if you followed my advice you'd net yerself a good life and a great home.' He sprawled himself across a fireside chair.

'If I'd followed your plans, Father, I'd still have been Kingsby's mistress until he threw me over for a wife of note. Daniel saw something in me neither you nor Caleb did. Now, I shall be a lady of the town, not one of the night, like my own father would have had me be! So what is it you want, Father?' She was standing at arm's reach away from him.

'You are not very polite to your Pa. If I'd married you off to Barnaby, a farmer's son, do you think you would have had all this? Eh, no, lass, you've been in the home of a gentleman and now you've got taste. After tonight I might be able to move in alongside; or perhaps, the cottage at the end of the street. I quite like that one, next to the Inn. Clara, you can relax, for your Pa's staying here a while . . .'

'How long's a while?' Clara asked sharply.

'You really know how to make a man feel wanted.' He stared at her, but she did not reply. Instead, she waited for him to answer. 'Just till the night comes then I'll be away. I need to be around town for a while. But you've not seen me, you hear me? If that woman in yer kitchen has any sense in that head of hers, neither will she say owt if anyone asks.'

'What are you up to, Father?' She saw him grin at her, pleased that he knew something she didn't. He was like a child, an evil one. 'Is Ma all right?'

'Always worried about Ma. Do you know what it is like raising a nest of women? You stick together and make a man feel unwanted. Why ever couldn't I have been given sons to raise.'

'Why, Father? So you could teach

them in a trade or just how to get drunk
and . . . '

He stood up and she immediately
took two steps back toward the door.
She always made sure that when Pa was
about, that he never managed to get
between her and the door. She was
quicker than him on her feet; even now,
dressed in her finery she could outrun
him. 'You watch that ungrateful mouth,
woman!' He leaned against her fireplace
and folded his arms. 'I've paid for the
cottage, your food and the clothes on
your back.'

'You! What about all the work me,
Faith, Ma and the girls do?'

'Now, you shut that face and show
me a room where I can kip for a few
hours and then I'll be away about my
business. Remember to tell that woman
that I've left and send her home early so
she don't know no better. There'll be
trouble tonight in town so stay in
and don't bother your head about it.'
He smiled, revealing his discoloured
uneven teeth.

'What trouble would that be?' she softened her voice.

'Let's just say that it's none of your business or concern. What you don't know can't hurt you.'

She reached into a drinks cabinet and brought out a bottle of French brandy. His eyes lit up instantly. Clara walked slowly over to him and placed a glass in his hand. 'Father, I do respect you but you worry us so.' She forced a smile and poured him a large glass of the spirit.

He took it, greedily gulping down his drink and sat back down.

'Do you need Daniel to help you? Is that why you're here?' she asked and saw the comfort that the drink gave him flush his face. She poured him another.

'Let's just say that after tonight, your ex-lover will be properly 'ex'.' He smiled, pleased with himself, oblivious to his own stupidity.

Clara refilled his glass and watched him gulp it down greedily. It was the bottle that Daniel kept especially at the back of the cupboard so she presumed it was his best. It certainly seemed to be strong as it had an instant effect on her father. She waited till he slipped into a daze of alcohol and then sleep. His arms wrapped themselves around his gut.

She replaced the bottle and locked the morning room door behind her as she left him there whilst she went to find Daniel. He would know what to do with him . . . but then she had a better idea. Perhaps it was time to do Caleb a favour. However, that would not solve her problem . . . or remove him permanently, or would it?

She walked quickly along the walkway towards the cooper's workshop. If Daniel was there, then she would ask him. If not, she would make her way towards the fort.

★   ★   ★

Daniel returned home annoyed. He had neither found Faith or his bloody father-in-law. It was no good. The man was a weight around his neck. He had roped him into this business with Gibbons and the Huthwaite man. They were powerful and had crossed his palm with more than a little silver, but things were getting out of hand. His own wife, his beautiful Clara, had nearly become caught up in the last meeting, and the stupid man had not even helped his own daughter, Faith, leaving her face down in the mud. He wanted a way to rid himself of Joseph, but how?

He thought that Clara was in the morning room but the door was locked, the key in the outside of the door. He turned and released the mechanism inside. Turning the handle slowly he felt for his knife which hung from his belt, covered by his coat. As the door swung open he saw Joseph sprawled hideously upon the floor.

Quickly, he closed the door behind him and locked it. He felt for Joseph's pulse, which was a futile gesture. He pulled the linen cloth from the walnut table and threw it over him. Daniel was scratching his head. What on earth had happened here and was Clara aware of it? Was she here? He left the room, found the servant in the kitchen busily preparing dinner.

'Sir, are you here for dinner?' she asked.

'Yes, yes I will be,' he answered her simply looking for any sign of distress in her behaviour, but there was none visible.

'Will Mr Berry be eating or did he leave before Mrs Dell, sir?' She stopped cutting the parsnip for a while whilst he hesitated.

'He's left. I did not realise he had been as I've just come in. You say Clara is out?'

'Aye, some minutes since, but she can't have gone far, sir, as she didn't take her muffler.'

Daniel made straight for the morning room and it was then he saw the glass which had rolled across the floor from the man's hand. He smelt the contents and slowly a smile crossed his face. 'You idiot, that's raw alcohol. You used the neat stuff.' Daniel had received a delivery of the finest, strongest spirit that had not been mixed, diluted, only coloured in order to disguise it. The man must have raided his store.

Daniel grinned broadly. He'd have to act quickly, but if his usual luck held up, then he'd be rid of his problem and his in-laws would be none-the-wiser. Tomorrow, he'd benevolently start offering them help and all those females would look to him as the head of the household. What's more, his Clara would be eternally indebted to him. Life could be good sometimes. Daniel worked swiftly to hide the body in the cellar until he could dispose of it during the cover of darkness.

14

Caleb felt Faith's warmth as he held her to him. She was so different to her sister. He didn't even want to compare the two but in his heart he realised that the dalliance with the elder would block any advances or show of interest he declared in his affections for the younger. Faith was respectable and an honourable woman who he could not help but admire. He'd seen the disgust and the determination in her face when she had overheard the local gentry discussing rather zealously their ideals for what should happen to her people. He shook his head as if to break his thoughts away from what had been to what was occurring now as her head that was nestled against his chest moved away and those, oh so innocent, sweet eyes looked helplessly upwards into his.

Faith could not believe what she had just said to this man. She stared into his eyes not knowing what he was thinking about her, presuming he was thinking her a child in comparison to her sister, Clara. She looked at the trees surrounding them and realised that they were on their own. She had to sort out her life, here and now.

'Major K . . .'

He interrupted her. 'Caleb, unless you wish me to address you as Miss Berry.'

She shook her head. 'Caleb, my father is involved with those people. He wishes you dead as do they. They are planning your murder I am sure. Caleb, you are in grave danger, as is the security of my family through my own father's ignorance and ill character. I can only imagine how you must despise my whole family, Caleb, but I can only try to assure you that we are not all lost causes.'

'I do not judge you, your mother, or your sisters on the deeds of your father and your elder sister. You have to believe me on this.'

Faith breathed more easily for she had been hoping he would say those words to her. 'Caleb, my father made Clara come to you. He wanted information. It was his fault that she became what she did.' Faith swallowed silently, for these were not easy issues for her to discuss with the man whom she admired so. She saw his face flinch slightly as her words sank in.

'You are telling me that your own father instructed his daughter to . . . ?' He shook his head unable to believe her words, or not wanting to. 'I've been a bloody fool, Faith! Now tell me what you have seen and heard and I shall try to amend the situation. But Faith, I will not have you caught up in the matter any more. You will be taken to the hall with your younger sisters and your mother, and I insist that all of you wait for me there. Whatever befalls your father, I give you my word that it will not cast a shadow on you.'

★   ★   ★

Flora looked at her two younger daughters playing outside the cottage. She sat down at the old wooden table on which she had rolled out a piece of pastry dough. Her flour-covered hands came together with such force that a cloud of fine mist rose from them. She washed them in her rinsing water and removed her apron. It was no good. She had let things go by unchallenged for years, happy with her daughters and glad her man left her alone. He sought the comfort of the inn, and she the comfort of her family and hearth, but now things had changed dramatically. He threatened to bring them all down. Not by making them poorer than they were already, but by destroying her family and her home, and that she could not abide the thought of. The Major was a gentleman whom she felt she could trust. She would go and talk to him. He'd tell her what she should do, and do it she would. Joseph Berry could go to hell, her daughters were her little angels and she would see them right.

★   ★   ★

Gibbons was not a happy man. He had waited for Berry to appear at the inn but he had not arrived. His instructions were clear. Tonight he had to watch a man burn down a stable block, in the process finishing off Caleb Kingsby, and then leave Berry's body at the scene. No trails back to Huthwaite. First, though, he had rabble to rouse so he downed his pint and went about his business.

★   ★   ★

James watched his major leave the abbey grounds without having entered the building at all. This was not what he was supposed to be doing so something had changed his friend's plans. He had also seen the girl, Faith Berry, talking to him. He was in the habit of watching his friend's back. He'd done it for years since the man had stopped a Corsair from skewering him on a battle field in a foreign land. The Major, then a lowly lieutenant had risked his life to save the soldier he had never met when his own unit had deserted him. In all their battles since, he had never really repaid him for it. One day he had promised he would, then he would return to his family in London. That time was near, for the Major could not be faulted in a fair fight, but this man, Huthwaite, and his side-kick, Gibbons, didn't play by fair rules. That didn't phase James — he had grown up in the Dials of London, he knew all types of fighting.

He saw the girl go first into the abbey and then return to Caleb. Now was his turn to act. He waited for the birds, or more aptly, vultures, to flee their nest; James would not dare to sully Holy ground. Instead, he waited quietly, watching. Relief lifted his spirits when the first rat, Berry, left, followed on by Gibbons. He thought that would be the end of them but was delighted when the king of the rats himself appeared on a fine mount from behind the abbey. Simeon did not bid the nun who waved farewell to him a greeting at all.

Simeon was riding through the woods heading for the south road. James realized the king of rats was going to take refuge in the safety of his own castle until his deeds were done by his minions. Then he would move in, and buy out what was left of the damaged mill or mine. James and Caleb knew all about the intended disruption at the mill — they had paid their spies well and even had a handful of carefully chosen ex soldiers working amongst the shift workers. Their orders were already in place and any resurgence would be quickly quashed, but these men were evil — they were bringing death upon the destruction. They wanted ownership but more than that even, they wanted rid of Caleb, and that gave James his chance to repay a longstanding debt.

He left Faith and Caleb together, knowing that he was going to follow the real threat. For the moment, he decided to leave Gibbons' trail and, instead, head away from town, following Simeon. He made his way through the trees, picking his way carefully around his prey. It was easy for him — previously a skirmisher in Wellington's army, he was proficient in his task. Simeon, who prided himself on his horsemanship, was no match for him in skill. James rode down onto the road and appeared through the trees ahead of him. He had a scarf around his face like a highwayman, pistol drawn and pointed at the man. They were remarkably inaccurate weapons but James guessed that Simeon would be too frightened and cowardly to risk a shot being let loose. A dark overcoat covered his uniform jacket.

Simeon stopped abruptly. He was holding the reins as if he was considering trying to make a break for it.

'I wouldna be doin' that, man.' James' heavy accent almost brought a smile to his own face but he did not want the man to realise he was Caleb's sergeant; if he did, he might gain confidence, and that would do his cause no good.

'If you want my purse, take it and be gone. I have a journey to complete.' He held out his purse and moved the horse forwards a step at a time. 'Take it and be gone, sir. You are no more than an inconvenience to me.'

The range was so close to James he could not miss his target. The man had more guts than he had bargained for.

'Take it, man. You know you want to.' Simeon was very confident, overly so, James thought, as if he knew something . . . too much. 'The Major cannot be paying his men enough if his sergeant has to double up as a highwayman. Or, perhaps you have seen the light and

146

want to change allegiances. I can make your life very comfortable. Once the Major is discovered tomorrow, or should I say once his remains are, the men in the militia will need a man to take over. I could make you that man. Think about it, a Major in your own army. What do you say, Sergeant James? Do we have a deal?' He shook the purse so that the coin inside jingled. 'You're tempted. I know men, they all have a price and I can tell you *are* tempted. Name your price.'

The shot rang out, Simeon's stunned eyes open wide as he fell to the ground. James jumped down long enough to collect the purse from him. 'Yes, man, I was tempted — to shoot you, and you tempted me too far.

He remounted his horse and headed off after Gibbons.

★ ★ ★

Caleb helped Faith remount the horse. He then climbed into the saddle behind her. 'Faith, there is something I would like to talk to you about. It just does not seem fitting here. I shall when this mess is sorted out, I promise. We are very alike in some ways. I feel that I . . . '

Faith had not travelled far with Caleb when she was distracted from his words by figures appearing further along the track. They were familiar figures. Flora and the girls were running along the road toward them.

'Ma! Ma!' Faith shouted and Caleb stopped the horse so that she could dismount. Faith ran toward her mother with her arms open wide. 'What's happened, Ma? I missed you so much, were you worried?'

'My lovely Faith. Such a good girl. Oh, you're safe.' She looked up to Caleb. 'Thank you, sir. With all my heart I thank you. You kept your word. I'll help you all that I can to break the trouble my husband has caused you, whatever his part in it. I'm so sorry. I apologise for him, he has no honour.'

Caleb had stayed seated on his horse.

'Make your way to my hall. You will be made welcome there. I have to go, Faith, we will have plenty of time to talk and become better acquainted when this business is done with.'

She walked back to the side of his horse. 'You will still want to know me after all that has happened?'

He looked at Flora. 'Excuse me, Ma'am.' Caleb leaned forward and kissed Faith full on the mouth. 'If you are willing, I should like to court you formally. I have only myself to consider as to propriety, Faith. My family are dead. I am my own man, but I should like to become yours also, in time. Not as with your sister,' his colour deepened slightly, 'that was unfortunate, possibly for both of us. For now, look after your poor mother, and your sisters. I will talk to you more of this later.'

He sat up, pulled the horse's reins before cantering away, breaking into a gallop.

Flora had tears in her eyes, whilst the girls giggled and blushed but, as for

Faith, she was so full of love of all types that she could not have been happier. Her mood only broke when in the distance a shot rang out and, in an instant, her manner changed and the moment was lost. She rushed her mother and sisters on down the road towards the town and hopefully to safety.

★   ★   ★

Clara returned home to find a stain upon her new rug. She was not at all pleased and had the maid take it away in disgust. Her father acted like an animal. She searched the house for him and was relieved that he had gone. Well, good riddance, she thought, and waited instead for her husband to return. Nightfall came and she was still waiting for him, so in a foul temper she took to her bed.

15

Daniel manhandled his father-in-law's body into an old coal sack from the cellar. Once he had his load balanced upon his shoulders, he lifted him with no problem at all. It was a cloud-covered night and that meant dark — no stars or moon visible to betray his actions. Dressed in black with a knitted cap covering most of his head, he carried his burden around the village towards Kemble Hall. He was about to reap his ultimate revenge upon Caleb Kingsby and rid himself of his ignorant father-in-law

* * *

Faith, her mother and the girls arrived at Kemble Hall, the small manor house that had been lovingly restored by Caleb over the previous year. They were shown in by a woman who answered the door. She had introduced herself as the house keeper and had prepared a large room for the family to stay in.

'I shall send up water, Mrs Berry, and a warm beverage.' The woman addressed Faith's mother, who appeared unable to speak.

'Thank you, Ma'am,' Faith replied for her. Her mother was staring at every flickering candle and lamp as the glow from them and the warm fire within the hearth cast light onto the large bed and chaise longue within the room.

'That's all right, miss. My name is Mrs Hemp, Philippa, if you prefer,' she answered, and walked to the door.

'Thank you, again . . . Philippa. I apologise for having kept you up so late.'

'No matter, I'll send up the drinks and some nibbles then I suggest you make sure that your mother and sisters catch their sleep. Tomorrow is another day to face.'

Faith nodded as the woman left them to acclimatise.

'Take off your shoes, girls. We mustn't make any marks on Mr Kingsby's lovely things.' Her mother's eyes watered as she walked over to Faith. 'Oh, lass, this man has a hankering for you. You consider seriously what the man is like and not what he can do for you. I think he is kind, but you must decide if it is the man or his home you find attractive.'

The two younger girls were rolling on the bed oblivious of their mother's conversation.

'I like him, Ma. I find him attractive and honourable. But we will need time. How can I even court a man such as he, with a fath . . . '

Faith stopped speaking because she never showed open disrespect of her father to her mother.

'I married your father. It is for me to deal with him. If Caleb can see you beyond his murky shadow, then leave your father to me. You live your life. I have made mine for better or worse.' Her mother hugged her tightly until the drinks and cold pastries arrived. Then all was excitement until each plate was clean and they were ready for their bed.

*   *   *

Gibbons waited in the shadows by the stables. Still the Berry man did not arrive. He had located a lamp and had a flint ready. This was not what it was supposed to be like, though. Then he heard movement in the bushes behind him. The man must be drunk, Gibbons thought, because he was headed for the hall. Gibbons approached from behind him realising that Berry was carrying something. What the hell was the man thinking of? Then he realised, he'd got Caleb over his shoulder.

'Berry, bring him here now. You're going too far!'

The figure stopped still and cautiously made his way back a few steps.

'Put him in the stables, man, and let's torch it as we planned.' Gibbons' gruff voice was unmistakable. He led the way back towards the edge of the stable block, the man he presumed was Berry following him. They stepped inside. Gibbons saw Berry's body being thrown down on the hay in the empty stall. He turned to see Daniel Dell standing next to him.

'He drank raw liquor and killed himself. I was going to burn him and the bloody hall together.' Dell spoke very low. 'So what's your instruction?'

Gibbons thought a moment. Simeon had told him to leave no witness. So he drew his knife and thrust it at Dell's side.

Dell saw the movement but couldn't move fast enough to avoid the weapon altogether. He staggered backwards feeling for his own knife. 'You bast . . . '

'Gentlemen, whatever has come between you?' James' voice brought both men's focus to his rifle barrel which was trained on Gibbons.

He placed his hand in his pocket and removed Simeon's coin purse. He tossed it to Gibbons who caught it in one hand, slightly bemused, but dropped it in his own pocket. Blood was seeping from Daniel's side.

'James, Berry drank himself to death. This man was going to burn down the stables, and I . . . '

'Need help, Daniel?' Caleb entered with two soldiers behind him. 'Take him to the kitchens and have Mrs Hemp look at that wound whilst you fetch him the doctor.'

One of the men helped Daniel to his feet. The fear in Daniel's face dripped away like his blood as he looked humbly at Caleb. 'Kingsby . . . Caleb . . . I'm . . . '

'We'll talk later, Daniel. But this ends here . . . no more!' Caleb's voice was sharp, adamant. Dell nodded and continued with aid to the hall.

'So what do we have here, James?' Caleb asked as the other soldier tied Gibbon's hands behind his back.

'When Mr Huthwaite hears of this . . . ' Gibbons began.

'What we have here, sir,' James spoke

boldly over Gibbons' lame threat, 'is a murderer, thief and would-be arsonist. If that isn't enough to condemn him we can add other charges in I should think.'

Gibbons' jaw dropped as he began to struggle with the soldier. His efforts met with derision.

'I found Simeon's body in the woods. I suspect you'll find the man's coin in Gibbons' pocket along with the flint he was going to use to torch the hall. Daniel headed him off here, and discovered Joseph's body. I suspect he was going to torch this and poor Berry at the same time when the men were busy over at the hall,' James finished and Caleb nodded understandingly at him.

Gibbons was struggling to protest, but the soldier had a firm hold on him.

'Take him to the cell. See if you can get the names of any of his accomplices and round them up, James.' Kingsby waited for the soldier to leave then turned to his friend.

'This is all very neat, James.' Caleb looked into the man's impassive eyes.

'Aye, lad, it is. Now you go see to Dell and your house guests and I'll tidy the business up here.'

As Caleb walked to the open air of the night he stopped and looked back at James. 'You'll need to give witness to all of this.'

'Aye, that I will.'

'Then will you be seeing your family in London?'

'Aye, that I will, but I'll return from time to time, if you'll be glad to see me.'

Caleb returned to him and gave him an uncustomary hug. 'Thank you, sergeant.'

He walked briskly out leaving the older man smiling broadly until he looked down upon Berry's body, then he scratched his head and returned to his night's work.

★　★　★

When Caleb returned to the hall, he went first to the kitchens and saw Faith administering to Daniel with Philippa.

'How is he doing?'

Faith looked over to him relieved that he was unhurt.

'He'll live, but he'll carry the mark as a reminder of his night out,' the housekeeper said as she finished wrapping a cloth bandage around him. 'Mr Dell, I'll show you to the room, then the doctor when he arrives will see if I'm right.' She helped him stand.

'Caleb, thank you . . . will you tell Clara for me?' He looked like a broken man to Faith, yet somehow better for it.

'Yes, in the morning.'

Faith and Caleb stood silently until Dell and Mrs Hemp had left them. Then she turned around and faced Caleb.

'He said Pa drunk himself to death.' Faith did not know what to feel. She was relieved but was struck with guilt that she could even think such thoughts.

'He is beyond earthly judgement now. So let him go and be glad that you have a good family and a roof over your head.'

He wrapped his arms around her and she him; both hugging for the need they felt in each other on such a cold heartless night, to feel the warmth and love of another living being.

He buried his face in her hair for a moment then kissed her with a passion that took away her breath and her pain.

'I nearly lost everything my solitary life possessed in one night, yet managed to come out of it, somehow, with not just a house but a home and a family to share it with.'

He sat her down on Mrs Hemp's chair and crouched near her. She could see how tired he was.

'Faith, will you stay here with your mother and sisters whilst we become better acquainted. Would you want to?'

Faith remembered what her mother had said and thought of the burden it would be to her if she had to lie to gain her family a better position in life, but as she looked into those deep brown eyes Faith had no doubts or qualms. She wanted to stay and become better acquainted with this man.

'Yes, Caleb. I will.' She heard a sigh escape his lips.

'Oh, woman, I thought your pause meant you were going to reject my offer.' He gathered her into his arms and embraced her.

'You should have more faith,' she whispered.

'With you here, I have quite enough . . . for now,' he replied quietly. He kissed her tenderly and she was filled by a wave of raw emotion. 'I shall court you, Faith Berry, like the gentle lady you truly are,' he spoke softly before sweeping her off her feet and carrying her to the landing outside her mother's room. 'Sleep well tonight, Faith, for tomorrow we shall start our future afresh.'

Faith watched as he descended the stairs, and smiled. Tomorrow would be like no other day, filled with promise and hope, but most of all love.

We do hope that you have enjoyed reading this large print book.

Did you know that all of our titles are available for purchase?

We publish a wide range of high quality large print books including:
Romances, Mysteries, Classics
General Fiction
Non Fiction and Westerns

Special interest titles available in large print are:
The Little Oxford Dictionary
Music Book, Song Book
Hymn Book, Service Book

Also available from us courtesy of Oxford University Press:
Young Readers' Dictionary
(large print edition)
Young Readers' Thesaurus
(large print edition)

For further information or a free brochure, please contact us at:
Ulverscroft Large Print Books Ltd.,
The Green, Bradgate Road, Anstey,
Leicester, LE7 7FU, England.
Tel: (00 44) **0116 236 4325**
Fax: (00 44) **0116 234 0205**